A SMATTERING OF
LATIN

Also available in the series:
A Smidgen of Shakespeare

A SMATTERING OF
LATIN

Simon R. H. James

PORTICO

First published in the United Kingdom in 2016 by
Portico
1 Gower Street
London
WC1E 6HD

An imprint of Pavilion Books Company Ltd

ISBN 978-1-91104-222-8

A CIP catalogue record for this book is available from the British Library.

10 9 8 7 6 5 4 3 2 1

Reproduction by Mission Productions Ltd, Hong Kong
Printed and bound by 1010 Printing International Ltd, China

This book can be ordered direct from the publisher at
www.pavilionbooks.com

CONTENTS

For the Love of Latin   7

FOR THE LOVE OF LATIN

Latin trains the brain. End of story.

That is the short response. As a Latin schoolmaster I frequently
come across accusations that my subject is 'boring' (in other words
difficult), 'irrelevant' and 'dead' … and not always just from the
pupils. But what good sport these challenges provide. Though many
mischievous observations from my youthful charges are often
without sound mind and judgement (they think 'dead' is a real
wind-up), others are indeed genuine and require a respectful reply.

Poor old Latin: it comes under assault from all kinds of *non
cognoscenti* who claim its anachronistic tendencies as an easy target
in these dark days of dumbing down.

You've read this far, however, so you should be interested in sharing
some of my ammunition, adding rigour to our defence against any
force seeking to undermine clear thought and spoil the fun.

Latin is difficult.

But more so is passing through the eye of a needle. The harder
something is, the greater the challenge. Give it a go. That rare 'click'
of a breakthrough, where once was confusion and darkness, is
revelatory. And once the light shines, one wonders what there ever
was to fear.

Latin is a supremely relevant language. It has survived for over 2500 years – an amazing feat by any measure you could deem worthy. Dominant during the Roman Empire, kept alive by the Church in the Dark Ages and then revitalized by the Renaissance and the invention of printing, Latin deserves more attention than it presently receives. It is omnipresent in archaeology, history, geography, geology, physics, chemistry, biology, botany, astronomy, art, law, religion, literature, music, language, technology and mathematics. Life is less confusing with a little Latin. And I have found it much clearer with a lot of Latin. The coming pages should illustrate this claim beyond question.

And as for claims to the language being 'dead'? Well, the answer is yes and no. Mostly no.

The language now known as Latin and studied in textbooks is the formal written version, so it has never been spoken. Except now that it is – since English has taken words such as post mortem, agenda, arena, exit, vertigo, et cetera and thousands of others as its own and given them a modern spin. The spoken version, commonly known as 'Vulgar Latin', is the one that has evolved and would have been far removed from the written stuff. Language, once spoken, enjoys flexibility in grammar, vocabulary and accent. Eventually it is liable to split itself into regional dialects. It is unlikely that a Gallic Roman would have ever understood a Turkish Roman, but, as with the standardized Chinese Mandarin of today, both could read the same newspaper.

In fact spoken remnants of Latin exist even now in the odd Swiss canton, in central Sardinia and in Vatican City, where it is the official language. Mass is conducted in ecclesiastical Latin. The Romantic languages French, Spanish, Portuguese, Romanian and Italian emerged from Vulgar Latin. Needless to say the study of Latin is a considerable help when learning these languages, but since at least 60 per cent of English is derived from Latin it is very useful here too.

Latin has proved an exceptional *lingua franca*. Until recently all documents and treatises were written in Latin, thus crossing all international borders without risking any offence between one nation and another. Now English has that role.

So why keep teaching Latin in schools? Its cultural output stands proudly alongside nations past and present. It has a wonderfully consistent grammar. And knowing one grammar thoroughly helps in learning other languages. Grammar offers precision, clarity of thought, fluidity and comprehension. There is no shame in trying to express oneself as clearly and succinctly as possible. Loss of language risks anarchy, and a lack of communication provokes a life without rules.

Latin's logic and structure truly demands discipline. It triggers thought, and young minds feed voraciously on clear answers. Show schoolchildren the finishing line and make it challenging enough to reach, and they will respond and beat all expectation.

Latin has certainly worked for some. Whenever any question arose over the intelligence of ex-England and Chelsea midfielder Frank Lampard, for instance, his A* in GCSE Latin came to his aid. At a higher level, others proficient in Latin were Winston Churchill, Benjamin Franklin, Teddy Roosevelt, Thomas Jefferson, Friedrich Nietzsche, Karl Marx, C. S. Lewis, Oscar Wilde and Gough Whitlam. More recently Boris Johnson has championed the Classics, Chris Martin of Coldplay has a degree in Latin and Greek and the internet entrepreneur Martha Lane-Fox studied Ancient History. Nick Owen and Martha Kearney of the BBC both studied Classics and Stephen Fry dabbles heavily. Mark Zuckerberg, the creator of Facebook, studied Latin and Greek at high school, and actor Tom Hiddleston has a Classics degree from Cambridge.

In short, Latin trains the brain.

1
LATIN IS
ALL AROUND

HARRY POTTER

It is well known that Joanne K. Rowling studied French and Classics at Exeter University, and it seems she put some of her time there to good use. Many of the spells, charms, curses and hexes incanted in the amazingly successful Harry Potter septilogy/heptalogy are a mixture of Latin and Greek, without paying too much attention to grammar. The Hogwart's motto *draco dormiens nunquam titillandus* ('a sleeping dragon should never be tickled'), in particular, attractively contains both a participle and gerundive of obligation. It is as fine a motto as any inspiring wizard would need to get through the day – along perhaps with a sip of *Felix Felicis*, first met in the *Half-Blood Prince*, to enhance one's luck for the day.

The following incantations are observed, more than once, in some or all of Rowling's seven epics:

1 Philosopher's Stone

2 Chamber of Secrets

3 Prisoner of Azkaban

4 Goblet of Fire

5 Order of the Phoenix

6 Half-Blood Prince

7 Deathly Hallows

Incantation
Book
Derivation
Effect

accio
4,6,7
accio (I summon)
summoning charm

aguamenti
6,7
aqua (water),
mens (mind)
issues water from
a wand

avis
4,6
avis (bird)
issues birds from a
wand

crucio
4
crucio (I torment)
causes extreme pain
(one of the three
unforgivable curses)

confundo
3,4,6
confundo (I confound)
causes perplexity

expecto patronum
3+
expecto (I await), *patronus*
(patron) summons a
personal guardian to ward
off dementors (non-beings,
as all fans will know)

**conjunctivitis
curse**
4,5
coniunctiva (of the eye)
damages eyesight

diffindo
4,6,7
diffundo (I scatter)
splits an object

fidelius charm
3,5,7
fidelis (trustworthy)
entrusts a secret to a
keeper

**finite
(incantatem)**
2,5,7
finio (I end), *incantatio*
(spell) breaks spells

expelliarmus
2+
expello (I expel), *arma*
(weapons)
disarms opponent

impervius
3,5,7
impervius (impassable)
repels substances

imperio
4,7
imperium (command)
controls victim's actions
(unforgivable)

incarcerous
5,6
carcer (prison)
traps with ropes

incendio
1,4,6
incendium (fire)
starts a fire

locomotor
5,7
locus (place), *moveo*
(I move)
levitates an object

legilimens
5,6
lego (I read), *mens*
(mind)
reads minds

levicorpus
5,6,7
levo (I lift), *corpus* (body)
dangles victim upside
down

locomotor mortis
1,6
as above, *mors* (death)
renders immobile

lumos
2+
lumen (light)
lights end of wand

morsmordre
4,6
mors (death), *mordeo* (I bite)
creates the Dark Mark

nox
3,7
nox (night)
puts out light at end
of wand

obliviate
2,7
obliviscor (I forget)
causes memory loss

protego
4+
protego (I protect)
provides a shield
against spell

petrificus totalus
1+
petra (rock), *totus* (whole)
causes victim's loss of
mobility

reducto
4,5,6
reduco (I lead back)
destroys objects

reparo
4+
reparo (I renew)
fixes broken objects

sectumsempra
6,7
seco (I cut), *semper*
(always)
slashes victim

rennervate
4,6
nervus (strength)
brings consciousness

riddikulus
3,4,5
ridiculus (laughable)
turns a boggart into
figure of fun

**wingardium
leviosa**
1,7
levo (I lift)
causes levitation

sonorus
4,7
sono (I make a noise)
amplifies a voice

tergeo
6,7
tergeo (I wipe)
cleans up

THE BEATLES

In 1995 Dr Jukka Ammondt, a Finnish teacher, gained praise for translating, performing and recording Elvis Presley songs in Latin. The titles included *nunc hic aut numquam* ('It's Now Or Never'), *non adamare non possum* ('Can't Help Falling In Love'), *cor ligneum* ('Wooden Heart'), *tenere me ama* ('Love Me Tender'), *nunc distrahor* ('All Shook Up'), *ne saevias* ('Don't Be Cruel') and *gaudi calcei* ('Blue Suede Shoes').

Surely it's only a matter of time before attention turns to The Beatles (*coleopteri*). So to get in first, here are title suggestions for all their official UK single releases…

AMA ME/AMES ME
'Love Me Do'

SI TIBI PLACET, ME DELECTA
'Please Please Me'

A ME, TIBI
'From Me To You'

EA TE AMAT
'She Loves You'

TUI MANUM TENERE VOLO
'I Want To Hold Your Hand'

(PECUNIA) NON POTEST EMERE MIHI AMOREM
'(Money) Can't Buy Me Love'

LONGI DIEI NOX
'A Hard Day's Night'

VALEO
'I Feel Fine'

TESSERA AD VEHENDUM
'Ticket To Ride'

ADIUVA!
'Help!'

**TANTUM PER UNUM DIEM
ADERAT/SOLVERE
POSSUMUS**

'Day Tripper/ We Can Work
It Out'

LIBELLI SCRIPTOR

'Paperback Writer'

**CROCEA NAVIS QUAE SUB
AQUA EST/HELENA RIGBY**

'Yellow Submarine/
Eleanor Rigby'

**VIA SESTERTIUS NOMINE/
FRAGORUM AGRI SEMPITERNI**

'Penny Lane/ Strawberry
Fields Forever'

**AMORE NOBIS OMNIBUS
OPUS EST**

'All You Need Is Love'

SALVE, VALE

'Hello Goodbye'

MATRONA MADONNA

'Lady Madonna'

IUDE

'Hey Jude'

**CARMEN IOANNIS
YOKONISQUE**

'The Ballad Of John And Yoko'

REDI

'Get Back'

ALIQUID/ IUNGITE

'Something/Come Together'

SIT

'Let It Be'

HERI

'Yesterday'

CARISSIMA, TE MODO CUPIO

'Baby It's You'

LIBER SICUT AVIS

'Free As A Bird'

VERUS AMOR

'Real Love'

LATIN IN THE CINEMA, PART I

The 13th Warrior (1999)

At the beginning of the film two Arabs from Baghdad meet a Viking party. How best to communicate? At the bidding of Antonio Banderas, Omar Sharif tries Greek; it appears understood as the Norseman replies in Latin, '*non loquetur quia mortuus est*': (Our king) will not speak with you as he is dead.

Absolution (1978)

Richard Burton has a rather unreasonable go at Dai Bradley who stumbles over his translation of '*his constitutis rebus, nactus*', especially the last word 'having obtained by chance'. These words are from Caesar's *Gallic Wars* Book IV.

An American Werewolf In London (1981)

Spread over the internet is an untrue rumour that Jenny Agutter's London flat is in Lupus Street, Pimlico because *lupus* means 'wolf' in Latin.

Atonement (2007)

Juno Temple plays on the name of Army Ammo chocolate bars for soldiers by reciting '*amo, amas, amat …*'

Boys Will Be Boys (1935)

While teaching a class about butterflies in a prison, Will Hay finds himself in an argument with an inmate over the origin of the word *Lepidoptera*. While the con suggests it derives from Greek, Hay insists it comes from Latin: *lepi* meaning butter and *doptera* meaning fly.

Braveheart (1995)

'*sanguinarius homo indomitus est*', kindly but rather loosely translated

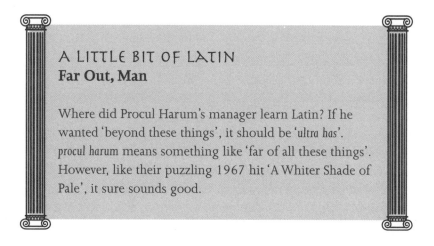

A LITTLE BIT OF LATIN
Far Out, Man

Where did Procul Harum's manager learn Latin? If he wanted 'beyond these things', it should be '*ultra has*'. *procul harum* means something like 'far of all these things'. However, like their puzzling 1967 hit 'A Whiter Shade of Pale', it sure sounds good.

in the subtitles as 'he's a bloody murdering savage', is spoken by one Englishman to another in front of Mel Gibson (William Wallace) to describe him. The speaker is unaware that the educated Wallace understands his words perfectly until he fashions a reply in the same secret tongue.

The Browning Version (1994)
Classics teacher Albert Finney quotes from Ovid's *ars amatoria*: '*ars est celare artem*' – the skill lies in how to hide the skill.

Candy (1968)
'*dulcis imperatrix*, whatever that may mean,' says Richard Burton in an address to an adoring audience. We can help you here, Richard: 'sweet empress'.

Carry On Cleo (1964)
Kenneth Williams translates his motto to clean up Rome, '*nihil ex pectore in omnibus*', as 'No spitting on public transport' – neatly anticipating the abbreviation of *omnibus* to bus by nearly 2000 years.

Carry On Henry (1971)
Sid James as Henry VIII utters his family motto 'non crapito suum januum', euphemistically translated as 'Don't spit on your own doorstep'. It is rather mangled Latin, as it should be tuam ianuam and crapito is made up.

Dead Poets Society (1989)
'carpe diem,' said the Roman poet Horace, 'because one shouldn't bet on tomorrow.' This was Robin Williams' philosophy to his English class. Oddly enough he had made a film called Seize The Day (1986) three years earlier. And there are in-jokes in other Williams films Mrs Doubtfire (1993) and Hook (1991).

Empire Of The Sun (1987)
Doctor Nigel Havers tests young Christian Bale with 'I shall love', 'They were being loved' and 'I shall have been loved' to keep up spirits in a Japanese internment camp. Bale later keeps himself going on a forced march by reciting the perfect indicative passive of amo.

Fear In The Night (1972)
Headmaster Peter Cushing plays recordings in his school of pupils reciting 'amatus sum, amatus es, amatus est...' The perfect indicative passive again.

Garfield 2 (2006)
The motto seen is 'adeo vices parum efficio'. Never translated, it could mean a number of things – perhaps 'I address changes, I accomplish very little'.

Girl Interrupted (1999)

When Vanessa Redgrave's patient Winona Ryder tells her doctor 'ambivalent' is her new favourite word, she replies that 'Ambivalence suggests strong feelings… in opposition. The prefix, as in ambidextrous, means both. The rest of it, in Latin, means vigour'. And she goes on with some Seneca, an excerpt from *Hercules Furens*, which she then kindly translates '*quis est hic locus? quae regio? quae mundi plaga?*' 'What world is this? What kingdom? What shores of what worlds?'

Goodbye Mr Chips (1939)

On his retirement Robert Donat quotes from Virgil's *Aeneid* Book I '*haec olim meminisse iuvabit*' ('Someday it will please to remember all this'). Back again as interim headmaster, Donat conducts a Latin class while all around bombs are falling. The lines for construing – what a splendid old-fashioned verb – are from Caesar's *Gallic Wars*, '*genus hoc est pugnae, quo se Germani exercuerant*' ('This was the kind of fighting in which the Germans busied themselves'). On hearing a correct translation from one of his pupils amid the mayhem, Donat says 'These dead languages do come to life sometimes, don't they?' to the merriment of all.

The Grass Is Greener (1960)

Cary Grant quotes Terence's '*nil dictum quod non dictum prius*' – 'there is nothing said that has not been said before'.

Greystoke (1984)

Note the Latin lesson Andie MacDowell (Jane) is giving Christopher Lambert (Tarzan). On the board is the future perfect of *amo*. No wonder, a cynic might observe, Tarzan could not wait to return to the jungle.

The Happy Years (1950)
Leo G. Carroll holds some very arid Latin classes at the Lawrenceville School, which Dean Stockwell attends. Three scenes stand out in which Carroll's blackboard has some Latin chalked, all impressively changing from one scene to another. Stockwell arranges with a classmate (who is able to wiggle his ears) to signal identification of gerund and gerundive, achieving a minor triumph over Carroll.

The Iron Man 2 (2010)
'Do you really speak Latin?' asks Robert Downey Jr. '*fallaces sunt rerum species*,' replies Scarlett Johansson, using a Seneca quotation, 'The appearance of things is deceptive'.

Lara Croft: Tomb Raider (2001)
Iain Glen, quoting Virgil, says to Daniel Craig, '*tempus fugit*', which Angelina Jolie then translates as the popular 'time flies'.

Lawrence Of Arabia (1962)
'Well, *nil nisi bonum*. But did he really deserve a place in here?' sniffs a clergyman attending Lawrence's funeral to Anthony Quayle, referring to St Paul's Cathedral. He is paraphrasing '*de mortuis nil nisi bonum dicendum est*', ('One should speak only good of the dead'), first quoted by Diogenes Laertius.

Man Without A Face (1993)
Disfigured teacher Mel Gibson's philosophy to his young pupil Nick Stahl is '*aut disce aut discede*': 'learn or leave'. Gibson asks Stahl to look up the Latin for his favourite attributive and he comes up with *excrementum*, while *puer stultus* is given to geometry problems. Later on a hike Gibson tests Stahl with '*quidam magistri discipulos tanta cum arte docebant ut ipsi a discipulis quidem discerent*', which Stahl never quite

finishes translating as 'Certain masters teach their pupils with such great art that they themselves indeed learn from their pupils'.

The Matrix (1999)
'*temet nosce*' appears above the door when Keanu Reeves visits 'the oracle'. *temet* is an emphatic form of *te*, hence 'Know thyself'. How wise. The original is inscribed on the Temple of Apollo at Delphi : γνωθι σεαυτον.

Monty Python's Life Of Brian (1979)
Romani, ite domum is the correct version demanded to be written out a hundred times by Roman centurion John Cleese, after Graham Chapman has painted the mural graffito *Romanes eunt domus*. Everything is wrong in Chapman's version: declension of noun, mood of verb and the lack of a case ending for *domus*.

My House In Umbria (2003)
'*carpe diem*,' yup that one again. Here Ronnie Barker advises Maggie Smith to live for the moment.

On Her Majesty's Secret Service (1968)
At the Royal College of Arms George Baker reveals to George Lazenby the Bond coat of arms, *orbis non sufficit* – which, of course, lends its title to *The World Is Not Enough*. Later, on the walls of Savalas' mountain lair, one can spot a coat of arms with the motto '*arae et foci*' (home and hearth). One can still see it to this day in the Piz Gloria above Mürren in Switzerland.

Paint Your Wagon (1970)
Stretching it, but listen to 'Gospel Of No Name City' ... 'Sodom was vice and *vice versa*. You wanna say where the vice was worser.'

Personal Affair (1953)
Mild-mannered schoolmaster Leo Genn gently chides a student for translating 'fert horrida iussa per auras' as Mercury 'carries horrid orders in his ears' — reading aures rather than auras 'through the breezes'. The line is from Virgil's *Aeneid IV* and the pupil is only one letter out.

Poseidon (2006)
Richard Dreyfuss orders an expensive bottle of wine with, yes, that one again, 'carpe diem'.

The Princess Diaries (2001) and The Princess Diaries 2 (2004)
The motto of Genovia, first seen briefly in the first film and a lot in the sequel, is 'totus corpus laborat'. Oh dear: this understandable error is rather indicative of the perception that everything is Latin should end '–us'. Unfortunately 'corpus' is a third declension neuter noun, so it should be 'totum corpus laborat' to mean 'the whole body works'.

Quo Vadis (1951)
The most famous version, as the others, takes its title from Peter's question to Jesus, 'Whither goest thou?' just before his crucifixion at Rome, as related in the apocryphal *Acts of Peter*. Jesus's reply is 'eo Romam iterum crucifigi' — 'I go to Rome to be crucified again'.

Seconds (1966)
Old buddies Rock Hudson and Murray Hamilton recognize each other after plastic surgery with the key words 'fidelis aeternus' — eternally faithful.

The Silence Of The Lambs (1993)
'quid pro quo. I tell you things, you tell me things,' says Anthony Hopkins to Jodie Foster and she iterates.

Tombstone (1993)

Unusual in a western, there is a witty trade of Latin aphorisms threateningly expressed by Val Kilmer and Michael Biehn in Wyatt Earp's bar. Kilmer starts 'in vino veritas'. You're drunk (Pliny). Biehn replies 'age quid agis.' A man's gotta do ... (proverb). Kilmer: 'credat judaeus Apella. non ego.' Who are you kidding? (Horace). Biehn: 'eventus stultorum magister.' You'll be wise after the event (Livy). Kilmer concludes: 'in pace requiescat.' You're dead (from the Latin Mass).

The Truman Show (1998)

'omnes pro uno, unum pro omnibus' ('All for one, one for all') is the motto of Seaside, Jim Carrey's television town in Florida.

Unman Wittering and Zigo (1971)

Newly hired schoolmaster David Hemmings reads out the school's motto 'docilitas proles auctoritas', which headmaster Douglas Wilmer translates as 'Authority is the child of obedience'. Not much obedience at this murderous school!

V for Vendetta (2005)

Natalie Portman reads out 'vi veri veniversum vivus vici', which Hugo Weaving correctly translates as 'by the power of truth, I, while living, have conquered the universe'. He then blows it by saying it comes from Faust by Goethe when it is thought it is from Marlowe's Doctor Faustus. John Standing chips in with a 'mea culpa'.

Victim (1961)

Sinister Derren Nesbitt threatens Dirk Bogarde with Juvenal's 'mens sana in corpore sano'.

The Wave (2008)
'*alea iacta est*,' Jürgen Vogel is told by Christiane Paul, when he wants to swop his autocracy class for Paul's anarchy class. So he makes his autocracy class far too popular for its own good instead.

Wayne's World (1992)
To Dana Carvey commenting on Tia Carrere with 'She's a babe', Mike Myers replies, 'She's a robo-babe. In Latin she would be called *babia maiora*.'

The Wizard Of Oz (1939)
Wizard Frank Morgan confers a degree of Thinkology from the *Universitatus Comitiatum e pluribus unum* (a very thinly veiled reference to the USA) to scarecrow Ray Bolger.

Young Winston (1972)
After perfectly declining *mensa*, Winston Churchill's famous bewilderment over the vocative case, especially when invoking a table, is re-enacted word for word as described in *My Early Life* by young Russell Lewis and headmaster Robert Hardy.

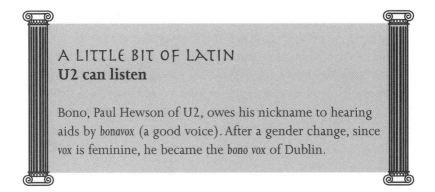

A LITTLE BIT OF LATIN
U2 can listen

Bono, Paul Hewson of U2, owes his nickname to hearing aids by *bonavox* (a good voice). After a gender change, since *vox* is feminine, he became the *bono vox* of Dublin.

ASTERIX

This endearing and enduring comic book series written and illustrated by Rene Goscinny (until his death in 1977) and Albert Uderzo frequently drew on well-known Latin phrases – usually untranslated and quoted by Roman legionaries, Julius Caesar and a particularly literate peg-legged pirate. Below is a selection of quotations from *Asterix* titles and the source if known.

Gaul *aut Caesar aut nihil* ('Either Caesar or nothing') Cesare Borgia's motto

Gaul *vae victo, vae victis* ('Woe to the vanquished man, woe to the vanquished men') Livy

Golden Sickle *vade retro* ('Get thee behind me') Terence and later St Mark's Gospel

Golden Sickle *acta est fabula* ('The story is done') Dying words of the Emperor Augustus

Golden Sickle *quis, quod, ubi, quibus auxiliis, cur, quomodo, quando?* ('Who, what, where, in what ways, why, how, when?') Quintilian

Goths *errare humanum est* ('To err is human') Seneca

Goths *video meliora proboque deteriora sequor* ('I see and approve the better ways, but I follow the worse ones') Ovid

Gladiator *singularis porcus* ('Wild boar') Linnaeus' classification

Banquet *exegi monumentum aere perennius* ('I have raised a monument more lasting than bronze') Horace

Banquet *victrix causa diis placuit, sed victa Catoni* ('The victorious cause pleased the gods, the defeated one pleased Cato') Lucan

Cleopatra *ita diis placuit* ('Thus it pleased the gods')

Big Fight *dulce et decorum est pro patria mori* ('It is sweet and fitting to die for one's country') Horace

Britain *fluctuat nec mergitur* ('It wavers but it does not sink') motto of the city of Paris

Britain *o fortunatos nimium, sua si bona norint agricolas* ('What fortunate farmers, if they only knew their good lot') Virgil

Normans *sol lucet omnibus* ('The sun shines for everyone') Petronius

Legionary *cogito ergo sum* ('I think therefore I am') Descartes

Legionary *dignus est intrare* ('He is worthy to enter') Moliere

Legionary *timeo Danaos et dona ferentes* ('I fear Greeks even when bearing gifts') Virgil

Chieftain's Shield *ab imo pectore* ('from the bottom of the heart') Caesar

Chieftain's Shield *bis repetita placent* ('Those things that please are rehashed again and again') Horace

Chieftain's Shield *diem perdidi* ('I have lost the day') – Titus bemoaning a wasted day

Chieftain's Shield *o tempora, o mores* ('What times! What customs!') Cicero

Olympic Games *et nunc, reges, intelligite, erudimini, qui iudicati terram* ('And now, kings, understand, be taught, you who have judged the Earth') – note the nice juxtaposition of active and passive imperatives from Psalms

Cauldron *ubi solitudinem faciunt, pacem appellant* ('Where they make desolation, they call it peace') Tacitus

Spain *beati pauperes spiritu* ('Blessed are the poor in spirit') St Matthew's Gospel

Spain *vanitas vanitatum et omnia vanitas* ('Vanity of vanities, all [is] vanity') Ecclesiastes

Roman Agent *auri sacra fames* ('The cursed hunger for gold') Virgil

Switzerland *maior e longinquo reverentia* ('Greater reverence from afar') Tacitus

Switzerland *nunc est bibendum* ('Now there's drinking to be done')
Horace

Mansions of the Gods *quousque tandem?* ('How long?') Cicero

Laurel Wreath *veritas odium parit* ('Truth begets hatred') Terence

Caesar's Gift *qui habet aures audiendi audiat* ('He who has ears, let him
hear') St Mark's Gospel

Caesar's Gift *de mortuis nil nisi bonus* ('[Say] nothing but good of the
dead') Chilon

Caesar's Gift *vinum et musica laetificant cor* ('Wine and music gladden
the heart')

Great Crossing *ira furor brevis est* ('Anger is a brief madness') Horace

Obelix and Co *redde Caesari quae sunt Caesaris* ('Render unto Caesar the
things that are Caesar's') St Matthew's Gospel

Obelix and Co *si vis pacem [para bellum]* ('If you wish peace, [be ready
for war]') Flavius Vegetius

Belgium *non licet omnibus adire Corinthum* ('Not everyone may go to
Corinth') Horace

Great Divide *nunc dimittis* ('Now you depart') St Luke's Gospel

Black Gold *non omnia possumus omnes* ('We cannot all [do] everything')
Virgil

Son *signa inferre! praege! concursu!* AD *gladios! infestis pilis!* ('Bring on
banners, forward, in a charge, to swords, with pilums at ready')

Magic Carpet *quot capita, tot sensus* ('As many feelings as heads') Terence

Magic Carpet *contraria contrariis curantur* ('Opposites are cured by
opposites') Hippocrates

Secret Weapon *desinit in piscem mulier formosa superne* ('A woman,
beautiful above, ends in a fishtail below') Horace

All At Sea *summum jus, summa injuria* ('the utmost enactment of law,
the utmost injustice') Cicero

Actress *ceterarum rerum prudens* ('Wary of everything else') Cicero
(adapted)

Class Act *res non verba* ('Deeds not words')

Falling Sky *nihil conveniens decretis eius* ('Nothing fitting to his decrees')
Cicero

Picts *verba volant [scripta manent]* ('Spoken words fly away [those
written stay]') Caius Titus

Missing Scroll *dat veniam corvis vexat censura columbas* ('The censor gives
pardon to the crows, he harasses the doves', i.e. the bad guys seem
to win at the loss of the good guys) Juvenal

A LITTLE BIT OF LATIN
Lorem ipsum forever

Ever seen text like this? *Lorem ipsum dolor sit amet, consectetur
adipiscing elit, sed do eiusmod tempor incididunt ut labore et dolore
magna aliqua. Ut enim* AD *minim veniam, quis nostrud exercitation
ullamco laboris ut aliquip ex ea commodo consequat.*
Don't even try to translate this. It is a load of old nonsense,
used to generate dummy or placeholder text for books so
that layout, as opposed to content, can be considered. It
has been used possibly ever since the advent of printing,
and actually hails from a real piece of Latin – namely
Cicero's *de finibus bonorum et malorum* (*'neque porro quisquam
est, qui do)lorem ipsum quia dolor sit amet, consectetur, adipisci velit,
sed quia non numquam eius modi tempora incidunt ut labore et dolore
magnam aliquam quaerat voluptatem'*). So lorem is dolorem, but
missing its head. The text then copies some of Cicero's
words, going on to muddle or misspell others.

Horace, *Odes* 3.29, lines 41–8

… ille potens sui
laetusque deget, cui licet in diem
dixisse, 'vixi'; cras vel atra
nube polum pater occupato
vel sole puro: non tamen irritum
quodcumque retro est efficiet. neque
diffinget infectumque reddet
quod fugiens semel hora vexit.

Happy the man, and happy he alone,
  He, who can call today his own:
  He who, secure within, can say
Tomorrow do thy worst, for I have lived today.
  Be fair, or foul, or rain, or shine
The joys I have possessed, in spite of fate are mine
  Not heaven itself upon the past has power;
But what has been, has been, and I have had my hour.

John Dryden (1631–1700)

BOOKS INFLUENCED BY THE ROMANS

In 1954 Rosemary Sutcliff wrote *The Eagle of the Ninth*, eventually filmed as *The Eagle* (2011), an enduringly good read. Another novel, *Song for A Dark Queen*, considers the Iceni queen Boudica, while *The Capricorn Bracelet* spans 300 years of life in Roman Britain. The prolific author Lynne Reid Banks took a harsh look at the circus in third-century AD Rome in *Tiger Tiger*, suiutable for older children. Other adult writers such as Colleen McCullough, Robert Harris, Lindsey Davis, Steven Saylor, Simon Scarrow and Conn Igulden have also published many books set in Ancient Rome. All have played valuable parts in a resurgence of interest in the classical world, especially for younger readers.

J. K. Rowling's *Harry Potter* series clearly delved into the classical world, notably with all the spells in Latin (pp.11–13). Dolores Umbridge is named after *dolor* (grief) and *umbra* (shade), and the vampire Sanguine after *sanguis* (blood). *Rufus* (red-headed), *Severus* (severe), *Regulus* (little king), *Lupin* (wolfish) and *Albus* (white) are straight translations. Draco Malfoy derives from *draco* (dragon) and his mother, Narcissa, is based on the vain Narcissus, venturing into the realms of Greek mythology. Narcissa's sisters are *Bellatrix* (female warrior) and Andromeda Tonks, while her husband is Lucius from *lux* (light); she is the daughter of *Cygnus* (swan) Black. Fluffy bears a strong resemblance to Cerberus, the canine guard of the Underworld, while Sirius Black is named for Orion's dog, both now a constellation. Minerva McGonagall comes from the Roman name for Artemis, and Sybill Trelawney from the Sibyl, the high priestess of Apollo. Argus Filch, the caretaker who, along with his cat, keeps an eye or two on the students is based on Argus the hundred-eyed giant.

The *Roman Mysteries* are a series of 17 history mystery novels, impeccably researched and written by Caroline Lawrence. Written for children, but also very satisfying for adults, they are set from AD 79 (the eruption of Mount Vesuvius) onwards. The books present a splendid take on Roman life, examining Roman mores as well as weaving in Greek myths, and frequently branch out from Ostia where the four young protagonists live. The BBC filmed the series in 2006 and 2007. Copies, signed by the author, receive certain Latin tags taken from, or inspired by, the stories. For example, number V, *The Dolphins of Laurentum*, has the tag *morbo medeor*, from *novum vetus vinum bibo novo veteri morbo medeor*. As described by Varro, this celebrates the vine harvest: 'I drink old and new wine, I am cured of old and new disease.' The book also includes an ingenious tag from XV Scribes from Alexandria — *tinea sum* 'I am a bookworm'. It is the answer to a riddle attributed to Symposius: *littera me pavit nec quid sit littera novi: in libris vixi nec sum studiosior inde; exedi Musas nec adhuc tamen ipsa profeci.*

> **I thrive on letters yet no letters I know.**
> **I live in books: but no more studious so,**
> **Though I devour the Muses, no wiser do I grow.**

Suzanne Collins' highly successful *The Hunger Games* is set in the state Panem, which provides games akin to gladiatorial combat. The name is taken from *panem et circenses* (Juvenal): 'As long as the emperor gives out free bread and puts on some good shows, the people will be appeased.' Its president, Coriolanus Snow, is named after the Roman general who also features in one of Shakespeare's plays. Romulus Thread keeps the peace violently in District 12. The gamemakers are Plutarch Heavensbee and Seneca Crane, after the celebrated Roman writers. Cinna was one of the conspirators who murdered Julius Caesar.

The logo of the *Cherub* series by Robert Muchamore resembles Cupid, the god of desire. Looking harmless, sweet and even cherubic, he nevertheless has arrows which sting with destructive

A LITTLE BIT OF LATIN
Shakespeare's Comedies

Impress your friends with erudite references to some
of the Bard's most engaging plays.

erunt bona omnia, si bene finient All's Well That Ends Well
ut vobis placet As You Like It
comoedia soloecismorum The Comedy of Errors
amoris labor perdita est Love's Labour's Lost
quid pro quo Measure for Measure
mercator Venetiae The Merchant of Venice
ludibundae uxores Windsoris The Merry Wives of Windsor
somnium intra noctem solstitii aestatis A Midsummer
Night's Dream
perturbatio multa pro nulla causa Much Ado about Nothing
viragonis domitura The Taming of the Shrew
tempestas The Tempest
duodecima nocte Twelfth Night
duo amici Veronae The Two Gentlemen of Verona
fabula, primo hiemalis, deinde per aestatem The Winter's Tale

madness, just like the agents. Meanwhile Eoin Colfer's Artemis Fowl
was named after the goddess of hunting. However, '… now and then
a male comes along with such a talent for hunting that he earns the
right to use that name. I am that male,' Artemis assures us. He is
quite pleased with himself – one of his aliases is Sir E. Brum
(*cerebrum*: the brain). The Fowl family motto is '*aurum est potestas*'.

An English teacher, Rick Riordan drew on mythology for his successful quintet of Percy Jackson novels. It is Percy's Latin teacher Mr Brunner (the centaur Chiron in disguise) who throws him a pen, which turns into a magical sword; this leads to the discovery that Percy is a demi-god, able to challenge the likes of the Minotaur, Medusa, Chimaera and Ares. There is some unforgettable Latin, as Percy yells at Mrs Dodds, '*braccas meas vescimini*' ('Eat my pants') – a variation of 'Eat my shorts', a catchphrase courtesy of Bart Simpson.

And there are many more. We could stray into the territory of Philip Pullman, Terry Pratchett, C. S. Lewis and even R. L. Stevenson's *Kidnapped*, which is not unlike the homecoming of Odysseus. But those are other stories…

LATIN TITLES OF WELL-KNOWN BOOKS

These are all suggestions should the books ever be translated into Latin – but some of them have already been published in translation. See Quiz V (pp.134-5) for the 'real deal'.

AQUILA NONAE LEGIONIS
The Eagle of the Ninth

EQUUS ATER PULCHERQUE
Black Beauty

HIRUNDINES ET MAMAE SINGULARES
Swallows and Amazons

HORTUS LATENS
The Secret Garden

EQUUS BELLI
War Horse

QUINQUE LIBERI ET ARENAE NYMPHA
Five Children and It

SOLEAE AD SALTANDUM
Ballet Shoes

**QUINQUE ITERUM
CONVENIUNT**
Five Are Together Again

THOMAS CURRUS TRACTORIUS
Thomas the Tank Engine

PUELLULA REDI DOMUM
Lassie Come Home

DOMINUS ANULORUM
The Lord of the Rings

LUDI FAMEI
The Hunger Games

ET DEINDE NULLUS ERAT
And Then There Were None

AQUILA AD TERRAM VOLAVIT
The Eagle Has Landed

FABULA DUARUM URBIUM
A Tale of Two Cities

BELLUM PAXQUE
War and Peace

FILII AMATORESQUE
Sons and Lovers

**RUBRUM TEMPLI,
SECULARIS ATER**
Le Rouge et le Noir

**GIBBUS VIR QUI SONAT
CAMPANAS NOSTRAE-FEMINAE**
The Hunchback of Notre-Dame

AVARITIA ET PRAECEPTIO
Pride and Prejudice

SOLITUDO CENTUM ANNOS
Cien años de soledad

MCMCCCIV
Nineteen Eighty-Four

Quiz I
THE BEST OF 00VII

Identify these James Bond Films. You will not need much help with deciphering these – though some of Ian Fleming's titles are a challenge even in English! The films are in chronological order, and include the two non-official titles.

medicus minime

a sinistra civitate (cum) amore

digitus auri

globus tonitrus

bis solum vivis

regius locus in quo ludi pecuniae tenentur

in servitudine secreto pro regina (I.S.S.P.R.)

pretiosae lapides sunt aeternae

vivet et moriatur

vir aureo telo

explorator qui me amabat

vir qui lunae imaginem removere conatur, i.e. is qui impossibile somnium petit

tuis oculis solum

animal cui sunt octo membra

numquam dic numquam iterum

consilium AD necandum/interficiendum

vivae luces diei

ei licet ut necet/occidat/interficiat

oculus aureus

cras numquam morietur

orbis terrarum haud satis est

morere alio die

regius locus in quo ludi pecuniae tenentur

minima quantitas solacii

e caelo casus

larva/idolon/umbra

Answers on page 151

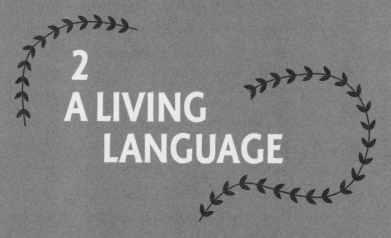

2
A LIVING
LANGUAGE

THE UNITED STATES OF AMERICA

In 1782, after six years of scholarly thought, a great seal was completed to commemorate the independence of the United States. The seal's obverse features the words '*e pluribus unum*' – meaning 'out of many, [states or peoples] one' [nation or people]. This phrase, attributed to Virgil, has been tracked back to the making of a pesto called *moretum*, in which lots of colours of different ingredients blend into one. The mottoes on the reverse definitely recall Virgil's work. From *The Aeneid* comes '*annuit coeptis*' ('He gave his approval to the undertakings'), while '*novus ordo seculorum*' ('a new order of ages') derives from the fourth *Georgic*. These mottoes can be seen today on the back of a US dollar bill, while *e pluribus unum* appears on all cent, nickel, dime and quarter coins.

Several American states have also adopted mottoes in Latin, with Maryland and South Carolina even taking two.

ARIZONA
regnat populus
The people
rule

ALABAMA
audemus iura nostra defendere
We dare defend
our rights

ALASKA
ditat Deus
God enriches
(inspired
by Genesis)

CALIFORNIA
εὕρηκα
I've found it
(Archimedes)
Yes, Greek but too
good to omit

CONNECTICUT
qui transtulit sustinet
He who transferred
sustains
(Psalms, adapted)

COLORADO
nil sine numine
Nothing without
divine will
(Virgil, adapted)

IDAHO
esto perpetua
Be perpetual
(originally
referring to Venice)

MAINE
dirigo
I guide

NEW YORK
excelsior
Higher
(Longfellow)

DELAWARE
iustitia omnibus
Justice for all
(last words of the
Pledge of Allegiance)

KANSAS
ad astra per aspera
To stars through
adversities (recalls
the RAF motto
per ardua AD astra)

KENTUCKY
Deo gratiam habeamus
Let's give thanks to God
Kentucky's motto was
only adopted in 2002,
so Latin lives on into
the twenty-first century

MARYLAND
*crescite et
multiplicamini*
Grow and
multiply
(Genesis)

MARYLAND 2
*scuto bonae voluntatis tuae
coronasti nos*
You have crowned
us with the shield of
your goodwill (Psalms)

MASSACHUSETTS
virtute et armis
With courage
and arms

MICHIGAN
si quaeris peninsulam amoenam circumspice
If you seek a pleasant peninsula, look around
(recalls the inscription to Christopher Wren
in St Paul's Cathedral, London)

MINNESOTA
*ense petit placidam sub
libertate quietem*
With the sword
she seeks peace
under liberty

OKLAHOMA
labor omnia vincit
Work conquers
all (Virgil)

OREGON
alis volat propriis
She flies with
her own wings

WEST VIRGINIA
montani semper liberi
Moutaineers are
always free

MONTANA
salus populi suprema lex esto
Let the welfare of the people be the supreme law
(also the motto of the London Borough of
Lewisham and can be found on the library in
Walworth Road, which is in Southwark)

NEW MEXICO
crescit eundo
It grows as
it goes

NORTH CAROLINA
esse quam videri
To be rather than
seem (Cicero)

SOUTH CAROLINA
animis opibusque parati
Ready in mind
and resources

SOUTH CAROLINA 2
dum spiro, spero
While I live,
I hope
(attributed to Cicero)

OHIO
imperium in imperio
Empire within an empire
Ohio's was very short-
lived, lasting only a
couple of years in the
nineteenth century

VIRGINIA
sic semper tyrannis
Thus always to tyrants
Apparently quoted by
John Wilkes Booth
when he shot
Abraham Lincoln

WYOMING
arma togae cedant
Let arms yield to
the toga (Cicero)

FOOTBALL MOTTOES

A few English and Scottish clubs in the Premiership, Championship and other divisions sport Latin mottoes on their club crests. These crests occasionally find their way into the design of players' shirts, though the money-making annual renewal of designs may mean the crest is omitted from one year to another.

Everton

nil satis nisi optimum
('nothing enough unless the best', i.e. only the best will do)
Note: this is similar to the Northern Irish side Ballyclare's motto *nihil nisi optimi*.

Arsenal

victoria concordia crescit
('victory grows from agreement', i.e. harmony breeds victory).
Note: *victoria* is nominative but *concordia* ablative (see chapter 6).

Elgin City

sic itur AD astra
('thus one goes to the stars', i.e. we aim high)
Note: *itur* is an impersonal passive from the verb *eo*. *astra* is accusative plural neuter, given away by the fact that AD governs the accusative.

Blackburn Rovers

arte et labore
('with skill and hard work')
Note: both nouns are third declension ablatives.

Tottenham Hotspur

audere est facere
('to dare is to do', i.e. daring is doing) Note: the verbs are infinitive, showing a nice classical preference to nominative gerunds.

Manchester City

superbia in proelio
('with pride in battle') Note: *superbia* is probably ablative, but could be nominative to mean simply 'pride in battle'.

Sheffield Wednesday

consilio et animis
('with a plan and minds', i.e. with wisdom and courage) Note: both nouns are ablative, *consilio* singular, *animis* plural.

Tranmere Rovers

ubi fides ibi lux et robur
('where faith there is light and strength', i.e. where there is belief, therein lies light and strength)

Bury

vincit omnia industria
('hard work overcomes everything') Note: the first declension noun *industria* is nominative singular, but *omnia* is accusative plural neuter.

Clydebank
labore et scientia
('by work and
knowledge')
Note: more ablatives.

Gillingham
domus clamantium
('house of those shouting',
i.e home to vocal support)
Note: *clamantium* is a genitive
plural present participle active
used as a substantive.
Now that's worth
shouting about.

Bristol City
vim promovet insitam
('promotes innate power')
This motto, shared with Bristol
University, is taken from Horace's *Fourth
Ode* which reveals that *doctrina* ('learning')
is the promoter of inner power. Note:
the adjective *insitam*'s –*am* ending
rather than –*um* reveals the noun
vim's gender to be feminine.

Mossley
floret qui laborat
('he who works flourishes')
Note: many mottoes rely
on a 'he who…'
translation for *qui* rather
than merely 'who'.

Queens Park
ludere causa ludendi
('playing for the sake of
playing') Note: observe the
neat contrast of infinitive
standing in for a nominative
gerund with a gerund in
the genitive.

Kilmarnock
confidemus
('we shall trust',
i.e. we trust)
Note: the verb is
future simple.

A LITTLE BIT OF LATIN
Getting Ink Done

Latin lends gravitas to one's body artwork. Modern tattooists are inundated with requests for ink in Latin.

David Beckham has several tattoos, two of them in Latin. One, under his Manchester United number VII, is *perfectio in spiritu* ('perfection in spirit') and another reads *ut amem et foveam* ('that I may love and cherish'). The latter has a couple of lovely, golden even, present subjunctives.

Angelina Jolie's tattoo along her waist is perhaps more sobering for the hedonist: *quod me nutrit me destruit* ('what nourishes me destroys me'). And in a similar vein Colin Farrell has used the old favourite *carpe diem* on his lower left arm.

ENGLISH COUNTY MOTTOES

The counties of England have been re-arranged over the centuries, most recently in 1965, 1974 and 1996, but the mottoes have by and large survived as counties come and go. Nicely summing up the confusion is Pembrokeshire, the sole Welsh county to have a Latin motto. It was merged into Dyfed in 1974, but returned in 1996 as Pembrokeshire with its motto *ex unitate vires* ('from unity strength') intact.

The following is a list of English county mottoes. Some are ceremonial; others are currently obsolete, but still may, one never knows, yet return.

BUCKINGHAMSHIRE
vestigia nulla retrorsum
no backward step
(adapted from Horace)

CAMBRIDGESHIRE
corde uno sapientes simus
with one heart let us be wise
per undas per agros
through waves, through fields
sapientes simus
let us be wise
Cambs has managed to procure
three grants of arms in all the
reorganization

CHESHIRE
iure et dignitate gladii
by right and dignity
of the sword

CUMBERLAND
perfero
I carry out

CUMBRIA
ad montes oculos levavi
I lifted my eyes to the hills

DERBYSHIRE
bene consulendo
by counselling well

DEVON
auxilio divino
with divine help

GLOUCESTER
prorsum semper
ever onwards

HEREFORDSHIRE
pulchra terra Dei donum
this beautiful land is God's gift

HUNTINGDONSHIRE
labore omnia florent
everything flourishes with work

KENT
invicta
unbeaten

LANCASHIRE
in concilio consilium
in council wisdom

LONDON, CITY OF
Domine, dirige nos
Lord, direct us

NORTH YORKSHIRE
unitate fortior
stronger united

NORTHAMPTONSHIRE
rosa concordiae signum
the rose is the sign of harmony

NOTTINGHAMSHIRE
sapienter proficiens
wisely advancing

OXFORDSHIRE
sapere aude
dare to know

RUTLAND
multum in parvo
much in a little

SHROPSHIRE
floreat Salopia
may Shropshire flourish

SUFFOLK
opus nostrum dirige
direct our work

Horace, *Odes* 1.4, lines 1–7

solvitur acris hiems grata vice veris et Favoni,
 trahuntque siccas machinae carinas,
ac neque iam stabulis gaudet pecus aut arator igni;
 nec prata canis albicant pruinis.
iam Cytherea choros ducit Venus imminente luna,
 iunctaeque Nymphis Gratiae decentes
alterno terram quantiunt pede.

Sharp winter now dissolved, the linnets sing,
The grateful breath of pleasing Zephyrs bring
The welcome joys of long desired spring.

The galleys now for open sea prepare,
The herds forsake their stalls for balmy air,
The fields adorned with green the approaching
 sun declare.

In shining nights the charming Venus leads
Her troop of Graces, and her lovely maids
Who gaily trip the ground in myrtle shades.

Lady Mary Wortley Montagu
(1689–1762)

UNIVERSITY MOTTOES

Educational mottoes are sometimes in Latin, often religious and always optimistic, in an attempt to grab the aspirations and imagination of their students. It sometimes works. Here are just a few British examples from the thousands over the world, including the *alma mater* of the odd prime minister (or several). See if you can spot them.

ABERDEEN
initium sapientiae timor Domini
fear of the Lord is the beginning
of wisdom (Ecclesiasticus)

BRISTOL
vim promovet insitam
promotes innate power (Horace)

CAMBRIDGE
hinc lucem et pocula sacra
from here [we drain] the light
and sacred cups [of knowledge]

CHESTER
qui docet in doctrina
he who teaches, on teaching
(Romans)

DERBY
experientia docet
experience teaches

DOWNING COLLEGE, CAMBRIDGE
quaerere verum
seek the truth

DUNDEE
magnificat anima mea dominum
my soul magnifies the Lord
(Luke)

DURHAM
fundamenta eius super montibus sanctis
her foundations [are] upon
the holy hills (Psalms)

EXETER
lucem sequimur
we follow the light

FITZWILLIAM COLLEGE, CAMBRIDGE
ex antiquis et novissimis optima
best out of old and new

GLASGOW
via, veritas, vita
the way, the truth, the life

IMPERIAL COLLEGE, LONDON
scientia imperii decus et tutamen
knowledge is the adornment and
protection of the empire

KING'S COLLEGE, CAMBRIDGE
veritas et utilitas
truth and usefulness

KING'S COLLEGE, LONDON
sancte et sapienter
with holiness and wisdom

LEEDS
et augebitur scientia
and knowledge will be increased

LEICESTER
ut vitam habeant
so that they may have life (John)

LINCOLN
excellentia per studium
excellence through study

LIVERPOOL
haec otia studia fovent
these leisure days foster learning

LONDON SCHOOL OF ECONOMICS
rerum cognoscere causas
to discover causes of things
(Virgil)

MANCHESTER
cognitio sapientia humanitas
knowledge, wisdom, humanity

MERTON COLLEGE, OXFORD
qui timet Deum faciet bona
he who fears God shall do good

NOTTINGHAM
sapientia urbs conditur
a city is founded on wisdom

OXFORD
dominus illuminatio mea
the Lord is my light (Psalms)

QUEEN MARY COLLEGE LONDON
coniunctis viribus
with united powers

QUEEN'S COLLEGE, OXFORD

nutrices tuae reginae erunt
queens will be your nursemaids
(Isaiah)

QUEENS' COLLEGE, CAMBRIDGE

floreat domus
may this house flourish

ROYAL HOLLOWAY (AND BEDFORD), LONDON

esse quam videri
to be rather than seem
(Cicero)

SALFORD

altiora petamus
let us seek higher things

SHEFFIELD

rerum cognoscere causas
to discover the causes of things

SOMERVILLE COLLEGE, OXFORD

donec rursus impleat orbem
until it should fill the
world again

TRINITY COLLEGE, CAMBRIDGE

virtus vera nobilitas
virtue is the true nobility

UNIVERSITY COLLEGE LONDON

cuncti adsint meritaeque expectent praemia palmae
let all be present and let
them await the rewards of a
deserved prize (Virgil)

WARWICK

mens agitat molem
the mind moves matter (Virgil)

WOLFSON COLLEGE, OXFORD

humani nil alienum
nothing alien to me as a human
(Terence)

YORK

in limine sapientiae
on the threshold of wisdom

Catullus, Poem 86

Quintia formosast multis; mihi candida, longa,
rectast. haec ego sic singular Confiteor,
totum illud formosa nego: nam nulla venustas,
nulla in tam magnost corpore mica salis
Lesbia formosast, quae cum pulcherrima totast,
tum omnibus una omnis surripuit Veneres.

Quintia is beautiful, many will tell you: to me
She is white, she is straight, she is tall: to all this
   I agree.
But does this make her beautiful? Though she
   be found without fault,
Can you find in the whole of her body the least
   pinch of salt?
But Lesbia is beautiful: hers is the secret alone
To steal from all beauty its beauty, and make it
   her own.

Arthur Symons (1865–1945)

TEXT ABBREVIATIONS AND WORDS

Many written works contain Latin phrases and words, often in an abbreviated form.

Here are some in current use:

Abbreviation	In full	Meaning
A.D.	anno domino	In the year of our Lord
a.m.	ante meridiem	Before midday
ante	–	Before (indicating an earlier passage)
c./ca.	circa	About/approximately
cf.	confer	Compare
cp.	compara	Compare
	erratum/errata	Error/errors
e.g.	exempli gratia	For the sake of an example (a relevant example to qualify a statement)
et al.	et alii/alia	And other people/things
etc.	et cetera	And the remaining things
fl.	floruit	He/she/it flourished (when a person was active)
ibid.	ibidem	In the same place (previously mentioned)
id./ead.	idem/eadem	The same man/woman
i.a.	inter alia	Among other things
i.e.	id est	That is (explains a statement)
N.B.	nota bene	Note well (particularly)

p.a.	per annum	Through a year (annually)
p.m.	post meridiem	After midday
p.p.	per procurationem	Through another (delegate) on behalf of someone
P.S.	post scriptum	After what's written (an addition)
Q.E.D.	quod erat demonstrandum	What was to be proved [has been]
q.v.	quod vide	Which see (look up elsewhere in current text)
post	–	After (indicating a later passage)
pro rata	–	In proportion
re	in re	In the matter of/concerning, now reborn in emails
sc.	scilicet/scire licet	It is permitted to know/that's to say (less used than i.e.)
sic	–	Thus (but may be wrong)
stet	–	Let it stand (don't change)
v.i.	vide infra	See below
v.s.	vide supra	See above
viz	videlicet/videre licet	It is permitted to see/namely (indicates examples)
v./vs	versus	Against

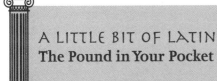

A LITTLE BIT OF LATIN
The Pound in Your Pocket

Current new pence boast in honour of Elizabeth II, D.G.REG.F.D, standing for *dei gratia regina fidei defensor* ('by the grace of God, queen and defender of the faith').

The edge of the English pound coin reveals *decus et tutamen* ('honour and protection'). The phrase sought to reassure that the coin was not clipped – as was frequently the case in the seventeenth century, when it first featured on a coin. The quotation comes from Virgil's *Aeneid V*, with the full line being '*donat habere viro, decus et tutamen in armis*'.

LATIN WORDS IN ENGLISH

No longer spoken, huh? Any of these words ring a bell?

abacus abdomen aborigines actor acumen addendum administrator agenda aggressor agitator album alias alibi altar alumnus amen animal animus annotator ante antenna anterior apex apparatus appendix aquarium area arena aroma asparagus assessor asylum auditorium aura axis basis benefactor biceps bonus cactus cadaver calculator camera campus caper captor caret caveat censor census cinnamon circus citrus clamour climax coitus collector colon colossus coma comma commentator compendium competitor compressor conductor consensus consortium continuum contractor cornucopia corpus cranium crater creator creditor credo crisis crux curator data decorum deficit delirium demonstrator dictator dictum dilemma diploma discus distributor doctor dogma drama duo duplicator echo editor educator ego elevator emphasis emporium enema enigma error exit exterior exterminator extra facile factor fiat focus formula forum fungus furore gemini genesis genius geranium gladiator gusto gymnasium habitat hiatus horizon horror hyena hyphen icon idea ignoramus illustrator imitator impostor impromptu incubator index indicator inertia inferior inquisitor insomnia inspector instigator instructor interest interim interior interrogator investigator iris item janitor junior languor legislator lens liberator liquor major mania martyr matrix mausoleum maximum mediator medium mentor minimum minister minor minus miser moderator momentum monitor moratorium motor murmur museum narrator nausea navigator nectar neuter nucleus oasis objector ode omen onus opera operator opus orator osmosis pallor panacea par paralysis pastor patina pauper pelvis peninsula perpetrator persecutor persona petroleum phoenix phosphorus plasma platinum plus podium pollen possessor posterior prior professor progenitor propaganda prosecutor prospectus protector quantum quota rabies radius ratio receptor recipe rector referendum regalia regimen renovator rostrum saliva sanatorium scintilla sculptor sector senator senior series serum simile sinister siren solarium species specimen spectator spectrum sponsor stadium status stigma stimulus stratum stupor successor superior tandem tenor terminus terror torpor transgressor translator tremor tribunal trio trivia tuba tutor ulterior vacuum verbatim vector vertigo vesper veto victor vigil villa virus visa vortex

… and many more.

A LITTLE BIT OF LATIN
Quality Advertising

A famous leisurewear firm decided that *mens sana in corpore sano* – a healthy mind in a healthy body – rather neatly embodied its philosophy. However, its name could not be MSICS, so they researched another word for *mens* and came up with *anima*.

Another firm wanted to call its raincoat a shield against water: *aquascutum* fitted the bill, and the rest is history.

The entrepreneurial, and perhaps meticulous, spirit of the Jameson family is represented on every bottle of Jameson Irish Whiskey: *sine metu* ('without fear').

And London's enduring emporium Harrods boasts *omnia omnibus ubique* ('everything for everyone everywhere').

RUDE LATIN

This is the naughty section for the intellectually curious, as well as those who may remember tormenting their Latin schoolmasters with inquiries such as, 'Sir, what's the Latin for six tall pine trees?' The answer, of course, is *sex erecti pinus*. Cue tittering.

So perhaps that's a good place to start.

Penis does of course mean penis, originally meaning a tail but soon losing it to accepted scientific appellation. More obscene is *mentula*, matching the female *cunnus*. The poet Catullus used this as a nickname. If erect or exposed by circumcision *verpa* was preferred, and Catullus uses the adjective *verpus*. He also mentions *sopio*, an enormous priapic caricature depicted in paintings such as those in the House of the Vettii in Pompeii, where it also appears in graffiti. Martial mentions the childish-sounding *pipinna* ('thingy'), and of course there is great potential for synonyms, such as the Latin for mast, flagpole and so on … you get the idea.

coleus ('*cojones*' is a popular word in Spanish) and *testis* are words for a testicle – the latter interesting in that one 'testified' in Roman courts by holding one's precious possessions. Cicero discusses both, among many other potential rude words, in his *epistulae* AD *familiares*.

The female *pudenda* (originally 'shameful' in Latin) is *cunnus*, later becoming *cunna* in a change of gender. It was quite an obscene word according to Cicero, who explains the curiosity of why Latin prefers *nobiscum* to *cum nobis* to mean 'with us', namely to avoid associations with *cunnus* in its ablative form (p.141). Horace blames Helen of Troy's 'bits' as the cause of the Trojan War. Sometimes the innocent *sinus* (fold) and *fossa* (ditch) could become synonyms, with the word *vagina* originally meaning a scabbard. Catullus and Martial mention *cunnilingus*, used unchanged today. The clitoris, *landica*, is evidently seriously forbidden as Cicero refuses to write it out, instead cleverly coming close with *illam dicam* ('I may say that thing') – but it does appear in Pompeiian graffiti.

clunis, culus (very popular as 'culo' in modern Italian and Spanish) are colourful words for the bottom, as is *anus* (ring). Unchanged *merda* is as popular in Italian as it was in Martial's day, though a more polite form (at least it appears in the Psalms) emerged as *stercus*. To produce such manure, the verb *cacare* (to defecate) has spread to German, Dutch and Russian, as well as enjoying its customary Romantic lineage.

Horace mentions *pedere* (to fart) in his *sermons*. In this word lies the origin of the intriguing phrase 'hoist with one's own petard', as quoted in *Hamlet* – though not so curious when one realises a petard was a bomb. *mingere* simply describes having a pee, while *meiere* can have connotations of ejaculation. The product of the former is *urina* or *lotium*, the latter related to *lavare* (to wash) through the Romans' use of ammonia of urine in their laundry.

Today's most popular four-letter word, *futuere* (to copulate), was equally a hit with Martial, Catullus and the graffiti artists of Pompeii. A personal favourite is the stark declaration of a long gone lady: *fututa sum hic* ('I got a good shagging here'). There seem to have been stronger words to match the aggression of today's favourite Anglo-Saxon monosyllabic utterance, for instance Catullus's *pedicabo* (literally 'I shall practice unnatural vice') and *irrumabo* (literally 'I shall treat obscenely'). Less graphic is the gentle *coire* ('to go with'), reflected in the current use of *coitus* in English. Martial came up with some further variations, using *cevere* for a male receiving male sex and *crisare* for a female receiving a male.

LATIN GRAFFITI

One of the happier results of Pompeii and Herculaeum's destruction
in AD 79 was the legible graffiti left for archaeologists. These were
recorded for posterity in the *Corpus Inscriptionum Latinarum*, first
published in 1857, which is just as well since, despite over 30
personal visits, these inscriptions remain difficult to make out.
Pompeii was in the grip of election fever, so much of it was political.
However, as we will see, some of the graffiti was more earthy and
not all that dissimilar to today's.

Here are some gentle ones.

LVCIVS PINXIT
Lucius painted this, i.e. Luke woz 'ere

OPPI, EMBOLIARI, FVR, FVRVNCLE
Oppius, you're a clown, a thief, a pilferer

EPAPHRA. GLABER ES
You're bald, Epaphra

HECTICE, PARVE, MERCATOR DICIT SALVE AD VOS
Hector, sweet, Mercator says hi to you.

These are slightly more specific.

DOMINUS EST NON GRATUS ANUS RODENTUM
the boss isn't worth a rat's arse.

MIXIMUS IN LECTO, FAETOR, PECCAVIMUS, HOSPES,
SI DICES QUARE, NULLLA MATELLA FUIT
we peed in the bed, I admit, we sinned, my host,
but if you ask why, there was no pot.

APOLLINARIS, MEDICUS TITI IMPERATORIS HIC
CACAVIT BENE
Apollinaris, doctor to the emperor Titus, had a good dump here.

Love (and lust) is never too far away.

SUSPIRIUM PUELLARUM CELADUS THRAEX
Thracian gladiator Celadus is the girls' heartthrob.

MARCELLUS PRAENESTINAM AMAT
ET NON CURATUR
Marcellus loves Praenestina, but it is unrequited.

LUCULLA EX CORPORE LUCRUM FACIEBAT
Luculla was profiting from her body. (Perhaps she wrote this.)

SUM TUA AERIS ASSIBUS II
I'm yours for two asses of bronze.

A political rivalry is also in evidence.

VATVAN AEDILES FVRVNCVLI ROG.
the thieves seek Vatia [to be elected] aedile

C. IVLIVM POLYBIVM AEDILEM ORO VOS
FACIATIS. PANEM BONVM FERT
I beg you to make Gaius Julius Polybius aedile.
He brings good bread.

Graffiti can be witty too.

ADMIROR, O PARIES, TE NON CECIDISSE, QVI TOT
SCRIPTORIVM TAEDIA SVSTINEAS
it's a wonder, o wall, you haven't collapsed, given so many
tedious inscriptions written on you.

FVLLONES VLVLAMQVE CANO,
NON ARMA VIRVMQVE
I sing of cloth-fullers and an owl, not arms and a man
[literary reference to Virgil here]

And this is impressive stuff.

NIHIL DVRARE POTEST TEMPORE PERPETVO;
CVM BENE SOL NITVIT, REDDITVR OCEANO,
DESCRESCIT PHOEBE, QVAE MODO FVIT,
VENTORVM FERITAS SAEPE FIT AVRA LEVIS.
Nothing can last forever.
As the sun shines, so it returns to the sea.
The moon, once full, wanes, ferocity of wind
often becomes a gentle breeze.

Horace, *Satires* 1.10, lines 14–15

ridiculum acri
fortius et melius magnas
  plerumque secat res.

Jesting decides great things
Stronglier, and better
  oft than earnest can.

John Milton (1608–1674)

Quiz II
NUMBER ONE HITS

Identify the hit records. All of the songs below have reached
Number One in the UK singles chart and received constant airplay
thanks to re-releases, covers, inclusion in films and advertising
use. The names of acts and years they reached the top (additional
dates for covers, where appropiate) are provided as enormous
clues. Some are literally translated, so further manipulation
may be required!

Year	Number One Hit
1953	*credo* (Frankie Laine; Robson & Jerome, 1995)
1954	*tres denarii in fonte* (Frank Sinatra)
1955	*'liberatum e vinculis' carmen* (Jimmy Young; Righteous Brothers, 1990; Robson & Jerome, 1995; Gareth Gates, 2002)
1956	*est paene cras* (The Dreamweavers)
1957	*erit ille dies* [in quo moriar] (The Crickets)
1958	*magni globi ignis* (Jerry Lee Lewis)
1959	*quid vis?* (Adam Faith)
1960	*solum soli* (Roy Orbison)
1961	*ad me recta redi* (Everly Brothers)
1962	*terra mira* (The Shadows)
1963	*quomodo id efficis?* (Gerry and the Pacemakers)

1964   domus solis orientis (The Animals); magnopere cepisti (The Kinks)

1965   i nunc (Moody Blues); mihi non satis est (The Rolling Stones)

1966   hae caligae factae sunt AD ambulandum (Nancy Sinatra); viridianae herbae domi (Tom Jones)

1967   hoc est meum carmen (Petula Clark); libera me (Engelbert Humperdinck); silentium est aureum (Tremeloes)

1968   quam orbem mirabilem (Louis Armstrong; Eva Cassidy & Katie Melua, 2007); mihi tibi nuntiandum est (Bee Gees); parvo auxilio ab meis amicis (Joe Cocker; Wet Wet Wet, 1988; Sam and Mark 2004)

1969   quo vadis, mea pulchra? (Peter Sarstedt)

1970   omnia genera omnium (Dana), anulus auri (Freda Payne)

1971   calidus amor (T. Rex)

1972   sine te (Nilsson; Mariah Carey, 1994); quomodo confirmari possum? (David Cassidy)

1973   flava vitta antiquam quercum circumligate (Dawn)

1974   illa (Charles Aznavour); quando iterum te videbis? (The Three Degrees)

1975   si (Telly Savalas); navigo (Rod Stewart)

1976   retine mihi omnia basia (Brotherhood of Man)

1977   itaque iterum vincis (Hot Chocolate)

1978   ter femina (The Commodores); aetatis noctes (John Travolta & Olivia Newton-John)

Answers on page 152

1979   *clari oculi* (Art Garfunkel); *nuntius in amphora* (The Police)

1980   *victor omnia vincit* (Abba)

1981   *mulier* (John Lennon); *nonne me cupis?* (Human League)

1983   *verus* (Spandau Ballet)

1984   *sciuntne diem natalem esse?* (Band Aid, also 1989, 2004)

1985   *volo scire quid sit amor* (Foreigner); *move propius* (Phyllis Nelson)

1986   *noli relinquere me hoc modo* (Communards)

1987   *iterum vincis* (Bee Gees); *quis est illa puella?* (Madonna)

1988   *is non gravis est, ille est meus frater* (Hollies); *tibi nihil debeo* (Bros);
        perfectus (Fairground Attraction); *Olympus est locus, qui est in terra*
        (Belinda Carlisle)

1989   *aeterna flamma* (Bangles; Atomic Kitten, 2001)

1990   *nihil te assimulat* (Sinead O'Connor)

1991   *omnia quae facio, pro te ago* (Bryan Adams)

1992   *finis viae* (Boyz II Men); *te semper amabo* (Whitney Houston)

1994   *ubique est amor* (Wet Wet Wet); *mane alium diem* (East 17)

1995   *villa* (Blur)

1996   *noli respectare, irate* (Oasis); *tres leones* (Lightning Seeds, again in
        1998); *vis esse* (Spice Girls); *verba* (Boyzone)

1997   *noli loqui* (No Doubt); *candela in vento* (Elton John),

1998   *numquam umquam* (All Saints); *cor meum supererit* (Celine Dion)

1999   *volans sine alis* (Westlife)

2000   *eheu … iterum egi* (Britney Spears)

2002   *si cras numquam adveniat* (Ronan Keating)

2003   *pulchra* (Christina Aguilera)

2004   *tibi faveo* (Girls Aloud)

2005   *adeone Amarillo?* (Tony Christie); *es bella* (James Blunt); *me tollis* (Westlife)

       mihi ridendum est (Lily Allen); *mihi saltare non placet* (Scissor Sisters)

       quingenta milia passuum (The Proclaimers); *fortior* (Kanye West)

2008   *clementia* (Duffy); *illud non est mihi nomen* (Ting Tings); *curre* (Leona Lewis)

2009   *pueri puellaeque* (Pixie Lott); *os sine expressione* (Lady Gaga)

2010   *scripta in stellis* (Tinie Tempah)

2011   *aliquis similis tibi* (Adele)

2012   *aliquis quem sciebam* (Gotye feat. Kimbra)

2013   *suffusae ligneae* (Robin Thicke); *incende* (Ellie Goulding); *clama ut leo fremit* (Katy Perry); *altissima aedes* (Sam Smith)

2014   *laetus* (Pharrell Williams); *canta* (Ed Sheeran)

2015   *detrahe me* (One Direction); *quid dicere vis?* (Justin Bieber)

3
LATIN
LOCATIONS

ENGLISH PLACE NAMES

Most English place names have origins in Celtic, Anglo-Saxon and Old English – and indeed in Latin, though many Roman names have long gone. The Roman city Deva, for example, has now become Chester, a name that also owes its origins to Latin.

Places ending in –cester, for example Bicester, Chester and Winchester, and in –caster, for example Lancaster, all derive from the Latin *castra* (a camp/ fortifications). A Roman legion built a camp in these places, which helped a settlement became permanent.

Ecclesia (church) is evident in Eccles, Lancashire, while *colonia*, as in *Lindum Colonia*, survives in the Anglo-Saxon name of Lincoln. London also seems to have hung on to its old name of *Londinium*. There are many settlements which retain elements of Latin today:

Latin	Meaning and English place
abbas	Abbot: Milton, Melbury, Compton (all Dorset)
ambo	Both: Lillings Ambo (Yorks) i.e. both West and East Lillings
canonicorum	Of the clergymen: Whitchurch Canonicorum (Dorset)
ducis	Of the duke or dukes (alternative nominative plural): Collingbourne Ducis (Wilts)
episcopi	Of the bishop (here of Bath and Wells): Huish (which means lands, not some mangled version of *hic*, *haec*, *hoc*) Episcopi, Kingsbury Episcopi (both Somerset)
extra and *infra*	Outside and within: Romsey Extra encircles Romsey Infra whose borders depend on a bridge (Hants)
forum	Market place: Blandford Forum (Dorset)
fratrum	Of the brothers: Toller (the river Toller is now called the Hooke) Fratrum (Dorset)
in fabis	In beans: Barton in Fabis, guess the village's produce (Notts)
inferior	Lower: Tabley Inferior (Cheshire)
intrinseca	Internal: Ryme Intrinseca (Dorset). John Betjeman's poem 'Dorset' begins 'Ryme Intrinseca …'

BLANDFORD FORUM

TABLEY INFERIOR

BARTON IN FABIS

iuxta/juxta	Close to: Norton Juxta Twycross (Leics), Bradford Juxta Coggeshall, Tilbury Juxta Clare (both Essex)
magna	Great: Appleby Magna, Stretton Magna (both Leics), Aston Magna, Compton Magna (both Glos), Hampton Magna (Warks), Chew (a river) Magna (Somerset), Fontmell Magna (Dorset)
monachorum	Of the monks: Buckland Monachorum (Devon)
parva	Small: Appleby Parva, Stretton Parva (both Leics)
porcorum	Of the pigs: Toller Porcorum (Dorset)
puerorum	Of the boys: Ashby Puerorum (Lincs) (found its name after a bishop assigned the church's revenue for the boys' choir in Lincoln cathedral)
sub	Under: Norton sub Hamdon (Somerset), Aston sub Edge, Weston sub Edge (both Glos)
super mare	Above the sea: Weston super Mare (Somerset) (but pronounced nowadays as the female horse rather than 'marr–ray')
superior	Upper: Tabley Superior (Cheshire)

NORTON JUXTA TWYCROSS

TOLLER PORCORUM

TABLEY SUPERIOR

APPLEBY MAGNA

ROMAN HOLIDAY

There are many Roman sites to visit in continental Europe and further afield. Here are a few suggestions, illustrating the width and breadth of Roman influence; some have been designated World Heritage Sites, while others remain undiscovered by mass tourism. Bridges, aqueducts, palaces, villas, forums, temples, theatres, amphitheatres, whole towns and museums await the adventurous – and although some are very well-known (almost too much so, given high season crowds), others are surprisingly overlooked and well worth an internet search.

Albania	Butrint
Algeria	Tipasa, Timgad
Armenia	Garni
Austria	Carnuntum, Flavia Solva
Azerbaijan	The site of the easternmost Roman inscription
Belgium	Tongeren, (Bavay, once in Roman Belgium, now France)
Bulgaria	Sozopol
Croatia	Pula, Split
Cyprus	Salamis
Egypt	Alexandria
France	Glanum (St Rémy), Grand, Pont du Gard, Nimes, Arles, Lyon, Fréjus, Orange, Nice-Cimiez
Germany	Hechingen-Stein villa, Regensburg, Saalburg, Waldgirmes, Porta Nigra (Trier)
Greece	Corinth, Olympia, Nicopolis, Thessaloniki (rotunda and arch of Galerius) – and many ancient Greek sites

Israel	Masada, Caesarea (for keen scuba-divers)
Italy	Rome, Pompeii, Herculaneum, Capri, Luna, Fiesole, Ostia Antica and Greek temples at Paestum. There are also many Greek and Roman remains in Sicily, including Taormina, Agrigento, Syracusa, Segesta and Piazza Armerina
Jordan	Jerash
Lebanon	Baalbek, Byblos, Tyre
Libya	Leptis Magna, Sabratha, Cyrene
Luxembourg	Echternach
Morocco	Volubilis
Portugal	Evora, Conimbriga
Romania	Tropaeum Traiani
Serbia	Gamzigrad-Romuliana
Spain	Numantia, Segovia, Merida, Tarragona, Sagunto
Switzerland	Vindonissa, Martigny, Aventicum. Augusta Rauonrica
Syria	Palmyra, Latakia, Bosra
Tunisia	Carthage, Dougga, el Djem
Turkey	Miletus, Myra, Ephesus, Pergamum, Didyma, Aphrodisias, Perge, Aspendos and many Greek sites, with possibly the lost city of Kane discovered in late 2015
USA	Las Vegas and Atlantic City (Caesar's Palace and Caesars respectively for the fake), Malibu (J. Paul Getty Museum for the real stuff)

A LITTLE BIT OF LATIN
Asterix's Gaul

Between 58 and 51 BC Julius Caesar fought the Gallic Wars, integrating most of modern-day France and Belgium into the Roman hegemony. All except one Gaulish village, that is. Asterix and his companions' indomitable stronghold was based in Armorica, also known as *Gallia Lugdunensis*, modern-day Britanny. Julius Caesar conquered this region in 56 BC, but his Gallic campaign was hard-fought. The Arvenians from *Arvenia* in the Auvergne region arose in 53 BC against Caesar, and in 52 BC their chief, the celebrated Vercingetorix, won a victory at *Gergovia* – a great victory much mentioned by Geriatrix of the village. At *Alesia*, however, he was forced to surrender to Caesar.

The Asterix adventures take place some time after this. Asterix and Obelix's parents live in *Condatum* (Rennes). Getafix's meeting place for druids in the Forest of the Carnutes was real, and is even mentioned by Caesar. *Lutetia*, the foundation of Paris, is held up as the urbane, glamorous and traffic-clogged city in contrast to the rural outpost in Britanny; it is the source of discord between chief Vitalstatistix and his wife Impedimenta. *Lutetia* is the second stop in *Asterix and the Banquet*, which provides a splendid tour of Gaul. It starts at *Rotomagus* (Rouen) and continues on through *Camaracum* (Cambrai), *Durocortorum* (Reims), *Divodurum* (Metz), *Lugdunum* (Lyon), *Nicae* (Nice), *Massilia* (Marseilles), *Tolosa* (Toulouse), *Aginum* (Agen), *Burdigala* (Bordeaux) and *Gesoribatum* (Le Conquet).

LATIN ALL OVER THE WORLD

As well as naming the provinces of their vast Empire, the Romans also managed to find names for territory beyond their conquests.

Latin name	Now known as
Albania	Georgia, Azerbaijan
Anatolia	Turkey (east)
Ariana	Afghanistan
Bithynia	Turkey (north-west)
Cambria	Wales
Colchis	Georgia
Helvetia	Switzerland
Hibernia	Ireland
Hispania	Spain
Islandia	Iceland
Lusitania	Portugal
Nubia	Sudan (north) and Egypt (south)
Numidia	Algeria
Parthia	Iran
Phoenicia	Lebanon
Ruthenia	Russia, Ukraine, Belarus
Sinae	China
Suecia	Sweden
Taporbana	Sri Lanka
Tingitania	Morocco

A LITTLE BIT OF LATIN
Great Stories of the Great

These witty examples of classically trained brains are
probably (and sadly) apocryphal.

Sir Francis Drake started the ball rolling upon
witnessing the flight of the Spanish Armada. He is reputed
to have quipped '*Cantharides*' – the medical name for the
aphrodisiac known as, wait for it … the Spanish fly.

Upon capturing Sind in 1843 General Sir Charles
Napier, he of the statue in Trafalgar Square, sent a one-
word dispatch to the Foreign Office, Governor General or
his brother, depending on the version one reads, '*peccavi*'
– 'I have sinned'. It is accepted that a *Punch* cartoon first
started this story.

Similarly in 1857 Lieutenant General Sir Colin Campbell
or Lord Clyde captured Lucknow during the Indian Mutiny
and was credited with the telegram '*nunc fortunatus sum*' –
'I am in luck now'.

Lord Dalhousie annexed Oudh in 1856 with the dubious
dispatch '*vovi*' – 'I have vowed'.

ROMAN SITES TO VISIT IN BRITAIN

There are hundreds of Roman sites in
England, and the following list is only
a selection. Many of the sites are run by
English Heritage or the National Trust.
A good day out beckons.

Aquae Sulis
The waters of the Celtic goddess Sulis,
whom the Romans associated with Minerva, were Roman baths
established in about AD 80 and used for over three centuries. They
were found in Bath in 1775 and now are one of the most spectacular
Roman sites in England. Highlights include a giant stone Medusa's
head and a bronze head
of Minerva herself.

Bignor Roman Villa
Bignor is close to Arundel in West Sussex and in its Roman heyday
boasted 70 buildings and over 40 acres. The remarkable villa here
was discovered in 1811. The museum contains an impressive array
of mosaics and the winter triclinium (dining room) features the
celebrated 'Venus and the Gladiators'.

Caerleon
Isca in South Wales has a massive legionary fortress, home to the II
Legion Augusta, together with a fine amphitheatre.

Chedworth Roman Villa
Discovered in 1864, a couple of baths and more mosaics can be
viewed at Yanworth near Cheltenham, Gloucestershire.

Dorchester

The Romans built this town *Durnovaria* as a capital for the Durotriges tribe to replace the nearby Iron Age Maiden Castle, a scene of supposed fierce fighting, suggested but not proved by a find of bodies.

Fishbourne

At Fishbourne on the Sussex coast, workmen digging a ditch in 1960 discovered Roman remains. Archaeologists proceeded to excavate over half of a sizeable palace. The north wing is uncovered and roofed over and open as a museum. Here one can see various archaeological treasures, including mosaic floors with hypocaust heating beneath, a skeleton, a boy's mask, a small ring suggesting that children lived there and charred door sills suggesting that there had once been a fire. In fact the fire destroyed the palace, which after being looted was forgotten for over 1000 years.

An inscription dedicated to Neptune and Minerva was discovered in the nearby city of Chichester, known in Roman times as *Noviomagus*. It was dedicated by Cogidubnus, or possibly Togidubnus, king of the Regnenses, a British tribe. It is now thought that the king was given the palace at Fishbourne as a reward for helping Emperor Claudius' invading army in AD 43.

Hadrian's Wall

Adopted by his predecessor Traianus or Trajan, Publius Hadrianus ruled as emperor from AD 117 to 138. He called a halt to Trajan's policy of imperial expansion, choosing instead to consolidate the defences in Britain, Germany and Numidia (in modern-day Algeria and Tunisia). Britain's wall, running from Newcastle to Carlisle, was built probably more as a tax collection point than a defence from marauding tribes as previously thought. The Gask Ridge, built 40 years earlier and much further to the north, may have had this job.

Three legions built Hadrian's Wall between AD 122 and 129. Incorporated into the wall were 16 forts, large enough to house 1000 men, and 79 towers known as milecastles; between each milecastle were two turrets used as lookout posts. The most famous sites of the wall are Housesteads and *Vindolanda*, both halfway along the wall and within spitting distance of each other. A further wall, known as the Antonine Wall, was added further north, built between AD 142 and 154.

Inchtuthil

A short-lived Roman fortress near Perth, Inchtuthil (called *Pinnata Castra* by the Romans) may have housed the XX Legion. Its occupants clearly left in an awful hurry, abandoning seven tons of valuable iron nails.

London

There is little left of *Londinium* after so much bombing and rebuilding in the capital. However, one can still see sections of the London Wall, the Temple of Mithras (moved to Queen Victoria Street EC4 in 1954, but possibly returning to its orginal site by the river Walbrook near Bank) and the remains of an amphitheatre under Guildhall Yard EC2. The Crossrail project unearthed numerous finds in Liverpool Street, and as recently as 2103 the river Walbrook has revealed leather shoes, among other items. They were discovered in Bloomberg Place EC4, which led the site to be dubbed the 'Pompeii of the North'. The Museum of London has a major Roman collection.

Lullingstone Roman Villa

This villa in Eynsford, Kent was discovered as recently as 1939, and was excavated from 1949. Destroyed by fire, the remains of the villa are now undercover. The *triclinium* mosaic is mythological, depicting separately Europa, whom Zeus abducted disguised as a bull, and Bellerophon, who slew the Chimaera.

Richborough
Rutupiae in Kent, now two miles inland, is thought to have been the spearhead of the Roman invasion in AD 43. There is an amphitheatre, a fort and the remains of a mighty triumphal arch.

St Albans
Known as *Verulamium*, St Albans was clearly an important trading and civic centre in Roman times. It is famous for the preservation of a rare Roman theatre.

Wall
An army staging post at Wall near Lichfield in Staffordshire, discovered in 1912, contains the remains of the *Letocetum* baths and a *mansio*. It is situated is on the important Roman road of Watling Street, which starts at London's Edgware Road and runs to Wroxeter.

Wroxeter
This was the old Roman city of *Viroconium*, found east of Shrewsbury in Shropshire. It boasts baths and a forum.

York
Eboracum was a major Roman town. It has remains of Roman city walls as well as excavations of baths, a temple and cemeteries outside the walls. The Yorkshire Museum in the city contains many Roman archaeological finds. To the northeast is the Roman road on Wheeldale Moor, part of the North Yorkshire Moors.

MONOPOLY IN ANCIENT ROME

Even though it was published back in 1935, Monopoly still has no Latin version. The one proposed below is based on ancient Rome, keeping to the spirit of the original board game. It offers at times fairly random choices of streets and areas, similar to those selected by Waddingtons, based in Leeds, for Parker Brothers.

Go *vade*; **Old Kent Road** *summoenium* (area outside the centre); **Whitechapel** *macellum Liviae* (shopping centre on the Esquiline)
King's Cross Station *porta Aurelia* (gate in the north-west)
The Angel, Islington *media subura* (like the Angel, an area rather than a street, famed for nightlife, between the Equiline and Viminal hills); **Euston Road** *via Appia* (first Roman road); **Pentonville Road** *alta semita* ('high path', passing over Quirinal)
Gaol *Tullianum* (the Mamertine prison named after Tullius, a legendary king of Rome)
Pall Mall *via sacra* (important central street); **Electric Company** *excubitorium vigilum* (barracks of firefighters); **Whitehall** *comitium* (political centre); **Northumberland Avenue** *vicus Iugarius* (runs along the Capitol)
Marylebone Station *porta Capena* (gate on via Appia on Caelian Hill running to south-east)
Bow Street *vicus Tuscus* (Etruscan central street near forum); **Marlborough Street** *clivus Argentarius* (as above); **Vine Street** *via nova* (as above)
Free parking *liberum spatium* (a free space)
Strand *argiletum* (street specializing in books); **Fleet Street** *vicus sandalarius* (as above, celebrating the former newspaper street);

Trafalgar Square *basilica Iulia* (court decorated with statues)

Fenchurch Street Station *porta salaria* ('salt' gate to north)

Leicester Square *circus maximus* (city's premium entertainment venue); **Coventry Street** *lacus pastorum* (pond of the shepherds, very random); **Water works** *cloaca maxima* (the main drain to the Tiber); **Piccadilly Circus** *miliarium aureum* (the forum's golden milestone, similar to 'Eros')

Go to gaol *vade* AD *Tullianum*

Regent Street *via lata* ('wide road,' now *via del corso*, very straight unlike Regent's bend); **Oxford Circus** *via Flaminia* (runs into the *via lata*); **Bond Street** *saepta Iulia* (enclosed public building near the *via lata*)

Liverpool Street Station *porta Esquilina* (the gate on the Esquiline to the east)

Park Lane *clivus Publicius* (near the *circus maximus*); **Mayfair** *mons Capitolinus* (the heart of Rome and smallest hill)

Chance *sors* (lot, fate); **Community Chest** (box of the state)

NB Importance of streets runs roughly in order of importance starting with *via, vicus, clivus,* down to *semita*.

VIA FLAMINIA	SAEPTA IULIA	SORS **?**	CLIVUS PUBLICIUS	MONS CAPITOLIN

Catullus, Poem 101

multas per gentes et multa per aequora vectus
advenio has miseras, frater, AD inferias.
ut te postremo donarem munere mortis
et mutam nequiquam alloquerer cinerem,
quando quidem fortuna nihi tete abstulit ipsum,
heu miser indigne frater adempte mihi.
nunc tamen interea haec. prisco quae more parentum
tradita sint tristi munere AD inferias,
accipe fraterno multum manantia fletu,
atque in perpetuum, frater, ave atque vale.

By ways remote and distant waters sped,
Brother, to thy sad grave-side am I come,
That I may give the last gifts to the dead,
And vainly parley with thine ashes dumb:
Since she who now bestows and now denies
Hath ta'en thee, hapless brother, from mine eyes.

But lo! These gifts, these heirlooms of past years,
Are made sad things to grace thy coffin shell,
Take them, all drenched with a brother's tears,
And, brother, for all time, hail and farewell!

Aubrey Beardsley (1872–1898)

D M
dis manibus
to the spirits
of the deceased

f [preceded
by letter]
filius
son of

DECIPHERING TOMBSTONES

Reading tombstones is a good way to show off your Latin knowledge
when visiting Roman sites – as long as you know some of the tricks.

On Roman tombstones the *praenomen* (first name) was an initial if it
was a common one; so was the father's. In this way, for example, Q
stood for Quintus, M Marcus, L Lucius, C Gaius, P Publius, T Titus,
D Decimus; there were also a few others. The *nomen* (clan name) was
given in full. One of 35 tribes to which a Roman citizen belonged

Q/M/L etc.
praenomina

LEG [followed
by numeral]
legio
legion

AN/ANN [followed
by numeral]
annorum
age

VIX
vixit
he/she lived

STIP [followed
by numeral]
stipendia
length of service

VETERAN/OPTIO
veteranus/optio
rank or
military status

was sometimes given, followed by the *cognomen* (surname), which
was given in full. The deceased's birthplace might be given in
abbreviation, followed by rank if he was a soldier.

Several of the same terms can be found on browsing through one's
local churchyard, as Latin was often used for the inscriptions. The
more Latin you know, the more you can understand about centuries-
old tombstones, which make valuable historical records.

H I (S)
hic iacet (sepultus)
here lies (buried)

H S E
hic situs est
is buried here

H F C
heres faciendum
curavit
an heir looked
after this burial

Quiz III
FAMOUS FILMS IN LATIN

Identify the cinematic hits. All the films in this quiz made an impact at the box office and are all well known. The accepted release year (or years in the case of remakes with identical titles) follow.

Giveaway parts of titles, for instance *Harry Potter*, *Indiana Jones*, *The Lord of the Rings*, *The Hobbit* and *Pirates of the Caribbean*, have been dropped, just to make it a little more challenging. Titles with an exclamation mark are taking a real liberty!

For example, I could have written *quiritatio sine oculo* meaning 'shriek without an eye', or even *quiritatio sine ego* meaning 'shriek without 'I'' in really bad Latin to get to *Shrek* (and even then there's the false alarm of *Scream*, hence the year to avoid confusion).

The Early Years of Cinema

Albus Niveus cum septem pumilionibus (1937); *egressus vento* (1939); *casa alba* (1942); *femina scelesta* (1946/1980); *tertius vir* (1949); *caerulea lucerna* (1950); *bellum mundorum* (1953/2005); *medicus adest* (1954); *et ego et rex* (1956); *decem imperia* (1956); *circum orbem terrarum octoginta diebus* (1956/2004); *dormiens pulchra puella* (1959).

The Sixties and Seventies

Maris undecim (1960/2001); *superbi septem* (1960/2016); *centum et uni canes* (1961/1996); *iuvenes* (1961); *trecenti* [Lacedaemonii] (1962/2006); *longissima dies* (1962); *mea pulchra femina* (1964); *iuva!* (1965); *sonitus carminum* (1965); *ubi aquilae audent* (1968); *o, iecur!* (!)

(1968); *fabula amoris* (1970); *vir qui obtulit aliquid quod non recusandum erat* (1972); *sellae equitationis incandescentes* (1974); *turris ignis* (1974); *dentes maris* (1975); *bella stellarum: spes nova* (1977) *pons plus* (1977); *ea quae non nata est in terra* (1979).

The Eighties and Nineties

imperium repugnat (1980); *currus ignis* (1981); *id quod non natum est in terra* (1982); *redite* AD *futurum* (1985); *optima hasta* (!) (1986); *improba saltatio* (1987); *ultimum iter pro bono* (1989); *vir qui est similis mammali noctis* (1989); *domi solus* (1990); *femina pulchra* (1990); *silentium agnorum* (1991); *hortus antiquorum animalium* (1993); *quattuor nuptiae funusque unum* (1993); *leo regius* (1994); *Romanus deus solis, tredecim* (1995); *maxima navis quae summersa est* (1997); *viri in vestibus nigris* (1997); *scriptor notus in amore* (1998); *mater* (!) (1999); *non in colle* (!) (1999); *sextus sensus* (1999).

The Noughties

illa quae feminae cupiunt (2000); *conveniamus parentes* (2000); *cubiculum celatarum rerum* (2002); *de puero* (2002); *heros araneus* (2002); *rex redit* (2003); *inveniens* 'no-one' (2003); *amor re vera* (2003); *arca mortui* (2006); *laeti pedes* (2006); *ludi senioris carmina* (2006); *expiatio* (2007); *crepesculum* (2008); *eques obscura* (2008); *mea mater* (2008); *iter per stellas* (2009).

The Twenty-Tens

inceptio (2010); *regis oratio* (2010); *celer quinque* (2011); *miseri* (2012); *gravitas* (2013), *frigidissimus* (2013); *proelium quinque exercituum* (2014); *quinquaginta glauci colores* (2015); *qui e mortuis rediit* (2016).

Answers on page 155

4
A LEARNED
LEGACY

LATIN AND THE LAW

Lawyers' Latin by John Gray provides a comprehensive cover to the treatment of Latin in legal use. Below are some of the more familiar legal phrases – unlikely to die out any time soon, despite some attempts to discourage their use. These then are the 'remnants of a residue', as Nicholas Ostler elegantly puts it in his ad *Infinitum*.

Latin	Translation
actus reus	Guilty act (the charge against the accused)
ad colligenda bona	To collect the goods [of the deceased]
ad hoc	To this [purpose] (decision to be made depending on the situation)
ad idem	To the same [opinion] (both parties agree on this point)
bona fide	In good faith (without the intention of fraud)
bona vacantia	Vacant goods (no-one entitled to an estate so the Crown gets it)

compos mentis	Composed of mind (i.e. sane), often used in the negative *non compos mentis*
corpus delicti	Body of crime (the body here being evidence)
de iure	By right
doli incapax	Incapable of crime
duces tecum	You will bring with you (a document to court)
ex gratia	Out of a grace (an award made without acceptance of blame
ex parte	By a party (when the other party is not present or notified)
habeas corpus	[A demand that] you have the body (writ to a custodian to produce prisoner before court to judge legality of detention)
ignorantia iuris non excusat	Ignorance of the law is no excuse (an unpermitted defence)
in camera	In the chamber (a private hearing)
in Curia	In open court (a public hearing)
in flagrante delicto	In the blazing act (caught red-handed)
in loco parentis	In the place of a parent (responsibility to act as a parent)
in personam	Against the person (an action against an individual)
in rem	Against the matter (an action directed against property or status on a non-specified person)
intra vires	Within the power [of the Court]
ipsissima verba	The very words
ipso facto	By that very fact (best understood in the example 'A blind person, *ipso facto*, cannot hold a driving licence')

mens rea	Guilty mind (the criminal intention)
mutatis mutandis	With the necessary changes [amendments] having been made
nulla bona	No assets (which can be seized from a guilty defendant)
obiter dictum	Something said in passing [by a judge and not constituting evidence or judgement]
per se	By itself
prima facie	At first sight (sufficient evidence, unless disproved, to prove a case)
pro bono (publico)	For the (public) good (used of voluntary work)
pro tem/pro tempore	For the time being
quasi	As if (not exactly what it might appear)
res iudicata	A thing adjudged (final decision on a case which cannot be re-raised)
res ipsa loquitur	The very thing speaks for itself (proof of the case is self-evident)
sine die	Without a day (a adjournment with a reconvening date held open)
sine qua non	Without which [it can] not [be] (i.e. an essential ingredient)
sub iudice	Under judgement (details of proceedings cannot be disclosed)
subpoena	Under a penalty (a writ directed to a witness to appear at Court)

A LITTLE BIT OF LATIN
E. L. Wisty Lives On

In the 60s revue *Beyond the Fringe* Peter Cook enjoyed a
hilarious monologue as a monotone miner and failed
judge, E. L Wisty. In the course of this he indelibly
established Latin as 'rigorous' – a tag that it has never really
lost. Here is an excerpt from one of his many versions:

> '… Yes I could have been a judge but I never had
> the Latin, never had the Latin for the judging.
> I never had it so I'd had it, as far as being a judge
> was concerned. I just never had sufficient of it to get
> through the rigorous judging exams. They're noted
> for their rigour. People came out staggering and
> saying 'What a rigorous exam,' and so I became a
> miner instead…'

ANY LATIN, WILL?

In his *Ode to Shakespeare* the playwright Ben Jonson declared that his celebrated contemporary William Shakespeare had 'small Latin and less Greek'.

Yet *Love Labour's Lost*, Act IV, scene ii would appear to disagree. Holofernes, speaking to Sir Nathaniel and Dull, comes up with *sanguis, caelo, terra, haud credo, in via, facere, ostentare, bis coctus, omne bene, perge, pia mater, mehercule*, translating all the while. On the entrance of Jaquenetta and Costard he utters '*vir sapit qui pauca loquitur*' – a wise man speaks little.

Next he quotes Mantuan, '*Fauste, precor, gelida quando pecus omne sub umbra ruminat* – and so forth'. This is from the first Eclogue of the late fifteenth-century poet Baptista Mantuanus. The quotation continues '*antiquos paulum recitemus amores*', meaning 'Please let's reminisce over lost loves, Faustus, while the cattle chew the cud in the cool shade'. Holofernes, however, carries on with *lege domine, caret, imitari* and reprises with *pauca verba*.

And finally we have more Latin in Act V, scene i, courtesy of Costard, 'For thou art not so long by the head as *honorificabilitudinitatibus*: thou art easier swallowed than a flap-dragon'. It is a very long word, subject to various anagrams attempting to prove or disprove Bacon's authorship of the play. It actually means 'by being able to achieve honours'.

So England's greatest literary genius seems to have enjoyed playing with Latin when it suited him. It appears again in the so-called 'problem play', *Measure for Measure*. Act V, scene i sees Lucio, in reference to Friar Lodowick's integrity, warn Escalus that 'cucullus non facit monachum' – a cowl doesn't make a monk.

The language also features in Shakespeare's history plays. In *Henry VI Part II* Lord Say utters 'bona terra, mala gens' (nice land, rotten people) – to which Jack Cade riposts with 'Away with him, he speaks Latin' (Act IV, scene vii). In *Henry VIII*, Act III, scene i Queen Katharine interrupts Cardinal Wolsey as he declares, 'tanta est erga te mentis integritas, regina serenissima' (there is such a great integrity of mind towards you, o most serene queen) – with the abrupt 'O, good my Lord, no Latin'.

In *Henry IV Part II* Pistol's almost Esperanto-esque 'si fortune me tormente, sperato me contente' (if fortune torments me, hope contents me) is not really Latin at all (Act II, scene v). By Act V, scene v, however, he manages 'tis semper idem for obsque hoc nihil est' – while obsque is a bit obscure, this seems to mean 'It's always the same for without this there is nothing'. In the same scene Pistol reprises in a slightly different form: 'si fortune me tormenta, spero contenta.' He's making it up as he goes along, isn't he?

Shakespeare also used his knowledge of gerundives when it came to creating a name for Prospero's daughter in *The Tempest*. Thinking perhaps of *Amanda* ('she who should be loved'), he came up with *Miranda* ('she who should be admired'). And Shakespeare, erudite chap that he was, drew on his Latin once again for Celia's alias in *As You Like It* – namely *Aliena* – a stranger.

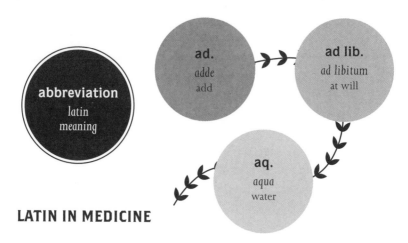

LATIN IN MEDICINE

There is still a tremendous amount of Latin in the field of medicine. It is a legacy of the time when all scientific documents were written in Latin to gain the widest possible circulation, as well as credibility among physicians.

In bones alone one will find *tibia*, *fibula* (brooch), *femur*, *ulna*, *radius*, *humerus* (funny bone), *patella* (little plate), *scapula*, *pelvis* (basin), *carpus*, *costa*, *os calcis* (bone of the heel) and *vertebrae*. Muscles meanwhile are *flexores*, *extensores*, *levatores* and *rotatores* according to function, for

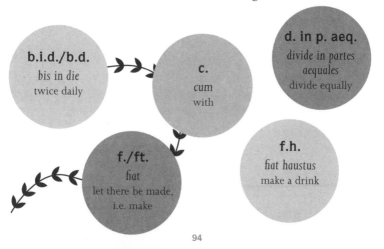

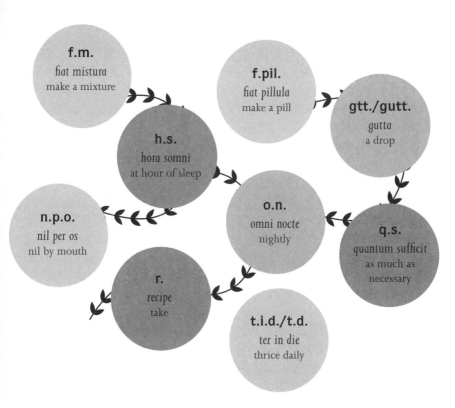

f.m.
fiat mistura
make a mixture

f.pil.
fiat pillula
make a pill

gtt./gutt.
gutta
a drop

h.s.
hora somni
at hour of sleep

o.n.
omni nocte
nightly

n.p.o.
nil per os
nil by mouth

q.s.
quantum sufficit
as much as
necessary

r.
recipe
take

t.i.d./t.d.
ter in die
thrice daily

example *flexores digitorum, extensor pollicis*. The principal vein is the
superior *vena cava*.

Latin abbreviations for prescriptions provide a good code, but it
can be cracked – if one can read the doctor's writing!

On the subject of body parts, the Romans had great fun with the
names of various fingers (*digiti*). The *pollex* is the thumb (and also the
big toe) while the *index* does the pointing. The middle finger is,
somewhat neutrally, the *medius* – or more controversially the *infamis*,
deriving from its time-honoured use in rude gesticulations. The
anularius, then as now, often wore a ring (*anulus*) and the little finger
was called the *auricularius*, judged most suitable for cleaning out the
ear wax of one's *auris*.

CHEMICAL SYMBOLS

Many chemical symbols were named from the Greek places and people, but others have Latin origins – thus explaining some of the seemingly bizarre symbols. Not all of the following elements were known to the Romans.

argentum **Ag** silver, money silver	alumen **Al** alum aluminium	aurum **Au** gold, shining dawn gold
cuprum **Cu** Cyprus metal copper	ferrum **Fe** iron, sword iron	Gallia **Ga** Gaul * gallium
magnes **Mg** magnet manganese	nitrum **N** native soda nitrogen	plumbum **Pb** lead, pipe lead
Ruthenia **Ru** Russia ruthenium	Scandia **Sc** Scandinavia scandium	silex **Si** flint silicon

origin
symbol
meaning
element

carbo **C** charcoa carbon	calx **Ca** lime, chalk calcium	caesius **Cs** sky-blue, grey-blue caesium
Hydrargyrum **Hg** [Latinized Greek] mercury	iris **Ir** rainbow iridium	kallium **K** [new Latin] potassium
natrium **Na** [new Latin] sodium	radius **Ra** ray radium	Rhenus **Re** Rhine rhenium
stannum **Sn** tin tin	stibium **Sb** antimony antimony	sulphur **S** sulphur, brimstone sulphur
		tellus **Te** earth tellurium

*The discoverer was a Frenchman, a Gaul, called Lecocq (the cockerel)

and the Latin for cockerel is *gallus*. Rather witty, all in all.

BOTANIC CLASSIFICATION

A big hooray for the Swede Carl von Linné, not only for adopting the very Romanesque name of Carolus Linnaeus, but also for establishing Latin (along with, to a certain extent, Greek) as the language of botany in the eighteenth century. His nomenclature in *Systema Naturae* distills the whole of nature as he knew it into the hierarchy of kingdoms, classes, orders, genera, species and varieties. Genus (e.g. *canis*) and species (e.g. *familiaris*) are the familiar make-up of a scientific name to form a library of hundreds of thousands.

Some of them are quite amusing as Richard Fortey points out in *Dry Store Room No. 1*, which laments that the mollusc *abra* lost its species *cadabra*. Duly revised, it was reassigned to a new genus to make the less memorable *theora cadabra*. But there's still *agra phobia*, *agra vation*, *apopyllus now*, *dissup irae*, *eubetia bigaulae* (say aloud in English pronunciation), *ittibittium*, *kamera lens*, *pieza rhea*, *ptomaspis dikenaspis ariaspis* (remove the *aspis*), *verae peculya*, *arses*, *silybum*.

One might wonder whether our eminent scientists are not taking nomenclature as seriously as they ought, while Latin names are abandoned for some entertaining puns. Not that Latin is devoid of it, of course, viz a recently extinct parrot called *vini vidivici* and the water beetle *Ytu Brutus*.

Here is a selection of some common Latin names found in British life, many taken from Paul Sterry's *Complete British Wildlife*.

MAMMALS

canis familiaris domestic dog
canis lupus wolf
felis catus domestic cat
felis sylvestris wild cat
glis glis edible dormouse
homo sapiens human being
lutra lutra otter
meles meles badger
mus musculus house mouse
mustela ermine stoat
rattus norvegicus brown rat
sciuris carolinensis grey
  squirrel
sciuris vulgaris red squirrel
vulpes vulpes fox

BIRDS

corvus corax raven
cuculus canorus cuckoo
passer domesticus house
  sparrow
picus viridis green woodpecker
riparia riparia sand martin
troglodytes troglodytes wren
turdus merula blackbird
turdus musicus song thrush

REPTILES

natrix natrix grass snake
vipera barus adder
caretta caretta loggerhead sea
  turtle
lacerta agilis sand lizard

AMPHIBIANS

bufo bufo common toad
rana temporaria common frog
triturus crestatus great crested
  newt

FISH

anguilla anguilla eel
salmo trutta trout
salmo salar salmon

INSECTS

apis mellifera honeybee
lasius niger black garden ant
musca domestica common
  house-fly
vespula vulgaris common
  wasp

TREES AND SHRUBS

acer pseudoplatanus sycamore
aesculus hippocastanum horse-
  chestnut
hedera helix ivy
ilex aquifolium holly
quercus robur English oak
taxus baccata yew

PLANTS

bellis perennis daisy
digitalis purpurea foxglove
galanthus nivalis snowdrop
urtica dioica nettle
viola odorata sweet violet

FRUIT

citrus sinensis orange
fragaria species strawberry
malus pumila apple
musa sapientum banana
pyrus communis pear
vitis vinifera grape

VEGETABLES

allium cepa onion
allium porrum leek
allium sativum garlic
brassica oleracea capitata
  cabbage
brassica oleracea gemmifera
  Brussels sprout
brassica oleracea
  italica broccoli
brassica rapa watercress
daucus carota carrot
pisium sativum pea
solanum tuberosum potato
spinacia oleracea spinach

Virgil, *Georgics* 2, lines 9–16

principio arboribus varia est natura creandis.
namque aliae nullis hominum cogentibus ipsae
sponte sua veniunt camposque et flumina late.
curva tenant, ut molle siler lentaeque genistae,
populus et glauca canentia fronde salicta;
pars autem posito surgunt de semine, ut altae
castaneae, nemorumque Iovi quae maxima frondet
aesculus, atque habitae Grais oracula quercus.

First, different trees have diverse birth assigned;
For some lack no compulsion of mankind,
But spring spontaneously in every nook,
Peopling the meadows and the mazy brook;
Thus osiers lithe, and brooms that gently play,
The poplar, and the willow silver-grey.
  And some arise from seed themselves have shed;
For so the chestnut rears its lofty head,
The bay-oak, towering monarch of the wood,
And oaks with Grecian oracles endued.

R. D. Blackmore (1825–1900)

CHURCH LATIN

Does this ring a bell?

> **salve, regina, mater misericordiae**
> **vita, dulcedo et spes nostra**
> **salve salve regina**
> **ad te clamamus, exules filii Evae.**
> **ad te suspiramus gementes et flentes**
> **o clemens o pia**

Fans of *Evita* will recognize this immediately as it comes from *Oh What a Circus* and was a hit for David Essex in 1978. It is a slightly truncated version of the first verse of *salve regina*, a Marian hymn sung

---

A LITTLE BIT OF LATIN
The Seven Deadly Sins

The Seven Deadly Sins were finalized by Pope Gregory I in AD 590, using biblical text from the book of Proverbs. They are *luxuria* (extravagance, lust), *gula* (gluttony), *avaritia* (greed), *acedia* (sloth), *ira* (wrath), *invidia* (envy) and *superbia* (pride). This list provided humorous inspiration for the film *The Magnificent Seven Deadly Sins* (1971) and, less appetisingly, for the killer of *Se7en* (1995), who based his serial murders on the sins. It also inspired the Japanese manga series 七つの大罪, which in turn became an anime series broadcast in 2015.

in the Catholic Church as well as being the final prayer of the Rosary. One can hear a later verse, jazzed up and conducted by Whoopi Goldberg, in *Sister Act* (1992). Other hit ventures by the pop world are Steeleye Span's 'Gaudete' and Enigma's 'Sadeness part 1'.

Ecclesiastical Latin, used in the Roman rite of the Catholic Church, is slightly different from Classical Latin. It sounds more Italianate.

This hardly needs translation.

> **Pater noster, qui es in caelis:**
> **sanctificetur Nomen Tuum;**
> **adveniat Regnum Tuum;**
> **fiat voluntas Tua,**
> **sicut in caelo, et in terra.**
> **panem nostrum cotidianum da nobis hodie;**
> **et dimitte nobis debita nostra,**
> **sicut et nos dimittimus debitoribus nostris;**
> **et ne nos inducas in tentationem;**
> **sed libera nos a malo. Amen**

Also familiar will be the Hail Mary, immortalized in music by Bach/ Gounod and others, but not to be confused, as it often is, with Schubert's version. The latter has a different lyric, though both are known as *Ave Maria*.

> **ave Maria, gratia plena, Dominus tecum;**
> **benedicta tu in mulieribus, et benedictus fructus ventris tui,**
> **Iesus.**
> **Sancta Maria, Mater Dei, ora pro nobis peccatoribus,**
> **nunc et in hora mortis nostrae. Amen**

Those who are not regular church goers will doubtless have heard the Gloria Patri in countless films, including *The Sound of Music* (1965), *The Godfather Part II* (1974), *The Name of the Rose* (1986), *We're No Angels* (1989) and *Seasons of the Witch* (2011).

Gloria Patri, et Filio, et Spiritui Sancto,
sicut erat in principio, et nunc, et semper, et in saecula
saeculorum. Amen.

To round off prayers, Mozart and Verdi, among many others, have set the Eternal Rest to music.

requiem aeternam dona eis, Domine
et lux perpetua luceat eis.
requiescant in pace. Amen

The Latinitas Foundation, established in 1976, has continued its work for use in The Vatican's affairs, keeping up with changes in the modern world. The Vatican even has a cash machine with instructions in Latin. The Foundation has published, both online and in two volumes, the *Lexicon recentis Latinitatis*, containing 15,000 new words such as bicycle (*birota*), cigarette (*fistula nicotiana*), computer (*instrumentum computatorium*), motel (*deversorium autocineticum*), popcorn (*maizae grana tosta*), rugby (*ludus follis ovati*), shampoo (*capitilavium*), strike (*operistitium*), terrorist (*tromocrates*), trademark (*ergasterii nota*), unemployed person (*invite otiosus*), waltz (*chorea Vindobonensis*). It also includes words unlikely to have much official use, such as flirt (*levis amor*) and hot pants (*brevissimae bracae femineae*).

Of course we are all still human, and even the Pope is reminded so during his coronation with the words *sic transit gloria mundi* (Thus passes away the glory of the world).

Medea's witchcraft
Ovid, *Metamorphoses* 7, lines 202–9

ventos abigoque vocoque,
vipereas rumpo verbis et carmine fauces,
vivaque saxa sua convulsaque robora terra
et silvas moveo iubeoque tremescere montis
et mugire solum manesque exire sepulcris!
te quoque, Luna, traho, quamvis Temesaea labores
aera tuos minuant; currus quoque carmine nostro
pallet avi, pallet nostris Aurora venenis!

By charms I raise and lay the winds,
    and burst the viper's jaw.
And from the bowels of the earth
    both stones and trees do draw.
Whole woods and forests I remove:
    I make the mountains shake,
And even the earth itself to groan
    and fearfully to quake.
I call up dead men from their graves:
    and thee, O lightsome moon
I darken oft, though beaten brass
    abate thy peril soon.
Our sorcery dims the morning fair,
    and darks the sun at noon.

Arthur Golding (1536–1605)

LATIN IN THE CINEMA, PART II

Time for the sequel. Let's take another trip to the cinema. All the films below have a flavour of the religious or supernatural.

The Awakening (2011)
'memento mori' is chanted at a séance which Rebecca Hall exposes as fake. This is 1921 and she takes a job to investigate a ghost at a school. Reading out the motto 'semper veritas', Dominic West replies, 'Latin gives a new school an air of respectability. It means they can add a pound to the fees'. 'I should imagine a bona fide ghost knocks it right off again,' Hall retorts. Later she reads on a schoolboy's desk 'ego contemno Latin. That you?' she addresses West as the banter continues.

Bedknobs And Broomsticks (1970)
'treguna mekoides trecorum satis dee', uttered by Angela Lansbury to bring inanimate objects to life, certainly sounds like Latin. However, apart from satis meaning 'enough', it is entirely meaningless.

The Da Vinci Code (2006)
'rhetor, omnes quattuor sunt mortui,' begins Paul Bettany on his mobile to his lords and masters of the Opus Dei in their preferred language. 'Teacher, all four (senechaux) are dead'… before ending with 'castigo meum corpus' and some grim self-flagellation to chastize his body.

Doctor Faustus (1967)
In the final scene Richard Burton reads from the rule book, i.e. the Bible, the famous legend, 'stipendium peccati mors est' – the wages of sin is death. It comes from Romans 6:23 and that wages plural jarring with a singular verb actually holds an iambic rhythm which the playwright Christopher Marlowe must have deliberately chosen.

Dragonslayer (1981)

Ralph Richardson intones a spell or two without great success at the beginning of the film trying to extinguish light with '*omnia in duos: duo in unum: unus in nihil: haec nec quattuor nec omnia nec duo nec unus nec nihil sunt*'. Co-stars Peter MacNicol and Chloe Salaman have a go at Latin as well, and all the spells are in Latin.

Event Horizon (1997)

A doomed space-captain left a crackly broadcast for his failed rescuers to decipher: '*liberate tute me ex inferis. ave atque vale.*' – deliver me from hell.

Excalibur (1982)

'*lacrimae mundi*, the tears of the world.' Nicol Williamson discusses the art of prophecy with Helen Mirren, using a line from Virgil's *Aeneid* I.

Father Brown (1954)

'*pax nobiscum,*' offers Alec Guinness when returned his bar of chocolate as the eponymous detective priest. He knows a little Latin as he later reminds Peter Finch while boasting of his motto '*optima semper libra sunt*', but is presumably polite enough not to point out the missing 'e' in "*libera*."

Ghost Rider (2007)

Peter Fonda as Mephistopheles offers a '*pactum pactorum*' for Matt Long to sign, essentially signing his soul over the Devil in exchange for his father's life. A drop of blood below the final line of the pact, which reads '*tibi animam meam in aeternam consecro*', seals the deal.

Hot Fuzz (2007)

Simon Pegg interrupts a meeting of the sinister village preservation society chanting 'bonum commune communitatis' – the common good of the community.

The Little Vampire (2000)
The film opens with Richard E. Grant chanting 'ab ovo, in toto, nil desperandum, sine die' – a set of four oft-used phrases, two of them by Horace. Meanwhile caveat vamptor (Let the vampire beware) is a mischievous play on caveat emptor. Jonathan Lipnicki has a vision of a crest 'sola animo at manuforti' – alone in spirit, but with a strong hand.

Night Of The Lepus (1972)
A lepus is a hare, and these are ungodly giant killers! Best categorized as cult fare.

The Omen (1976)
Remember the scary Gregorian chant? The words, as far as I can make out, are 'sanguis, bibimus, corpus, edimus, tolle corpus Satani ave, ave ave versus Cristus' – 'the blood, we drink, the body, we eat, raise the body of Satan, hail, hail, anti Christ'. All rather grim.

The Passion Of The Christ (2004)
All of the dialogue in this film, which was co-written, produced and directed by Mel Gibson, and deals with the last hours of Jesus' crucifixion by Pontius Pilate in the AD 30s, is in Aramaic and Latin.

Sebastiane (1976)
Derek Jarman shot the whole of his film, depicting the martyrdom of Sebastiane in the third century AD, entirely in Latin. Hardly family viewing, the reason why most of the cast parade around naked is because the budget could not stretch to Roman uniforms. Other

films made in Latin are *carmina burana* (1975), *Barnabus and Bella* (2010), filmed in Santa Monica, and *The Roman* (2014).

The West Wing
To finish with, here is an episode from television's *The West Wing* entitled 'Two Cathedrals'. In this US President Jebediah Bartlett (Martin Sheen) delivers a sarcastic rant against God in a cathedral:

'*gratias tibi ago, Domine. haec credam a Deo pio, a Deo iusto, a Deo scito. cruciatus in crucem. tuus in terra servus, nuntius fui: officium effeci. cruciatus in crucem. eas in crucem.*'

'Thanks a lot, Lord. Am I to believe these acts came from a righteous God, a just God, an omniscient God? Go to hell. I have been your servant, your messenger on this earth. I did my duty. Be crucified on the cross. May you go to hell.'

Quiz IV
NUMBER ONE POP ARTISTS

Identify these pop groups and solo artists. All have reached
Number One in the UK singles chart between 1952 and 2015 at
least once. To help, each act is listed under the year it first hit
the top spot. These are, or were, all popular acts and artists.
The Number One Hits section (pp.64–67) contains most of these
as further clues.

Hint: Under 1955 could have come *pelvis sine piso preme partum* (!),
i.e pelvis without a pea press meadow/lea so Elvis Presley. But that
was a bit contorted (hence the exclamation mark) and *pelvis* rather
gave it away, anyway.

The *coleoptera*, or possibly that should be the less mellifluous
sounding *scarabei*, have been allotted their own section in chapter 1
(see pp.14–15).

porta est dies (!) (1954); *textores somniorum* (1956); *cicadae* (1957); *semper pratum fratres* (1958); *umbrae* (1961); *exquisitores* (1963); *animalia and saxa volventia* (both 1964); *fratres iusti, petitores, ilices aquifoliae, aves and apricus et divide* (!) (1965); *fratres qui ambulant, vultus parvi and pueri litoris* (all 1966); *simii qui litteras ordinare non possunt* (1967); *aurora, media via and necatus* (1971); *novi petitores* (1972); *decem vide vide* (!) (1973); *limus and tres adiunctivae quantitates* (1974); *regina* (1975) *hiems, ver, aestas, autumnus and res vera* (1976); 'lion' *orator and alae* (1977); *vicani incolae and vigiles* (1979); *primus vir et formicae and hominum foedus* (1981); *currisne? currisne?* (!) and tu, *age quadraginta* (1983); *stellarum navis* (1987); *madidus, umidus, udus and tu quoque* (1988); *novi iuvenes in via and animi stulti* (1989); *australis pulcher* (1990); *a pueris* AD *viros* (1992); *tene illud* (1993); *princeps* (1994); *arbores circum aquam in deserto* (1995); *puellae cibi acris* (1996); *totaliter beatae* (1998); *gradus and Britannum genu hastae* (1999); *dulces infantes* or perhaps *mellis bellissimae* (2002); *fractus and proclivis restire* (!) (2003); *viae* (2004); *femina insane* (!) (2009); *flue, eques* (2010); *exemplum and valles* (!) (2011); *florea et machina* (2012); *auferens stultus and voluntas.ego.sum* (2013); *paulum mixtae* (2015).

Answers on page 158

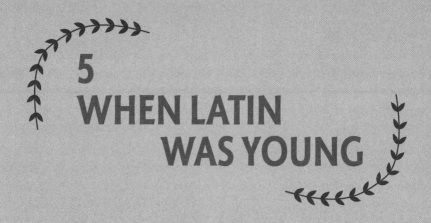

5
WHEN LATIN
WAS YOUNG

KEY EVENTS IN THE ROMAN REPUBLIC

Here is a potted history covering major Roman occurrences in the years BC (Before Christ), before Rome became an empire.

At approximately 1100 BC, the legendary Aeneas arrived in Italy after escaping from Troy. He proceded to found Alba Longa, not too far from the river Tiber, on the site where Romulus and Remus later built the city of Rome. The foundation date was later set by Varro as 21 April 753 BC. Three years later Romulus, the first king, directed the rape of the Sabines.

   After he was carried up to the heavens at roughly 716 BC, a succession of kings followed: Numa Pompilius, Tullus Hostilius, Ancus Martius, Tarquinius Priscus and Servius Tullius. In 510 BC the seventh king, Tarquinius Superbus, was banished by his nephew Brutus, duly appointed by the senate as one of the first two consuls. So the Roman Republic was established, which endured for the next 500 years; Tarquinius was finally seen off at the battle of Lake Regillus in 496 BC. The 12 tables, which gathered earlier codes and traditions, established a foundation of Roman law in 450 BC. At the battle of Veii in 396 BC Furius Camillus defeated the Etruscans, only

to be exiled for his troubles. In 387 he was
recalled to dispatch the Gauls after Manlius
and hissing geese saved the Capitol.

The dominant age of the patricians thus came to
an end. Plebeians were permitted to stand for the
consulship, dictatorship and praetorship during the
300s BC. In 312 Appius Claudius began the 132-mile Via Appia
linking Rome and Capua, literally paving the way for Roman
domination of Italy: it was finally completed in 264 after the defeat
of Pyrrhus, a major Greek opponent of Rome, at Beneventum.

Carthage was the next problem for Rome, confronting the
Republic in three Punic Wars. In 218 BC Hannibal crossed the Alps,
and after victory at Lake Trasimene and Cannae in successive years
Maharbal told him *vincere scis; victoria uti nescis*. And indeed Hannibal
never followed through by capturing Rome; he was defeated at
Zama back in Tunisia in 202 by Scipio 'Africanus'. At the end of the
Third Punic War in 146 BC Carthage was destroyed. Greece came
under Roman control and the Mediterranean belonged to Rome.

Internal pressures on the Republic led to a series of Social and
Servile Wars between 135 and 71 BC. The slave Spartacus led a
famous revolt, holing up on Mount Vesuvius in 73 BC, but two years
later 6000 slaves were hanged on the Appian Way. Powers were
allotted to the triumvirate of Crassus, Pompey and Caesar (p.124)
for various campaigns against pirates (Pompey), the Parthians
(against whom Crassus lost his life at Carrhae in 53 BC) and Gaul –
and, to a lesser extent, Britain (Caesar). After Caesar's assassination
Antonius and Octavian hunted down the perpetrators at Philippi in
42 BC, then set about each other. In 30 BC both Antonius (Antony)
and Cleopatra, queen of Egypt, committed suicide after the battle of
Actium the previous year. By 27 BC Octavian had become Augustus
and the Republic was at an end.

THE EMPERORS

Shortly before the birth of Jesus Christ the Roman Republic collapsed and became an empire. For the next century the emperors – well chronicled by writers such as Plutarch, Tacitus and Suetonius – provided a rich source of inspiration for modern popular culture – not only in cinematic epics, but also on television. The latter examined the subject chronologically in *The Caesars* (1968) and *I Claudius* (1976), based on Robert Graves' novel *I Claudius* and its sequel *Claudius the God*. This BBC production proves, over 30 years later, to contain the strongest portrayal, especially that of Derek Jacobi: it is still almost impossible for anyone else to override his powerful identification with the role. *Anno Domini* (1985) and more recently *Rome* (2005–7) have kept new audiences well fuelled with the nefarious machinations of Roman emperors.

There follows a brief history of those emperors, along with a selection of their screen appearances.

Augustus (Octavian) (27 BC–AD 14)
Gaius Octavius, born in 63 BC, was sensible enough to be adopted by Julius Caesar to become Gaius Julius Caesar Octavianus. He was an ally of Marcus Antonius (Mark Antony) when the two defeated Caesar's assassins Cassius and Brutus at Philippi, but the coalition proved short-lived. Antony had become over-friendly with Cleopatra, the Greek queen of Egypt, whom Julius Caesar had also admired. Octavian defeated Antony in the naval battle of Actium in 31 BC, after which Antony and Cleopatra committed suicide and he was able to obtain complete power.

In 27 BC Octavian changed his name to Augustus and became emperor (which Caesar never was); he did not call himself emperor, but instead *princeps* (first citizen) or *primus inter pares* (first among

equals – a somewhat oxymoronic phrase much beloved over the ages and providing a title for Jeffrey Archer's novel). Augustus dramatically increased the *imperium Romanum* and protected his position by cutting down on the number of legions, increasing military service and establishing the Praetorian Guard. Poets Virgil and Horace, his contemporaries, were kind enough to immortalize his period of rule as the 'Golden Age', while Augustus blew his own trumpet with *res gestae*.

Augustus has been portrayed on the screen by Ian Keith in *Cleopatra* (1934), Bob Holt in *Julius Caesar* (1950), Douglas Watson in *Julius Caesar* (1953), most famously by Roddy McDowall in *Cleopatra* (1963), Richard Chamberlain in *Julius Caesar* (1970), John Castle in *Antony and Cleopatra* (1972) and Albert Lupo in *Son of Cleopatra* (1964). On television he features in *The Caesars* and *I Claudius*, portrayed respectively by Roland Culver and Brian Blessed.

Tiberius (AD 14–AD 37)
Tiberius became emperor after Augustus in AD 14, but virtually retired to Capri in the Bay of Naples, leaving Sejanus, an untrustworthy sidekick (who eventually had to be executed), to deal with the intrigues at Rome. The remains of his palace at Capri, called *Villa Iovis*, are situated at the top of a sheer cliff from where, it is said, much amusement was gained by pushing unfortunates over the edge.

Tiberius has been portrayed by Cedric Hardwicke in *Salome* (1953), Ernest Thesiger in *The Robe* (1953), Hubert Rudley in *The Big Fisherman* (1959), George Relph in *Ben-Hur* (1959), Peter O'Toole in *Caligula* (1979) and Max von Sydow in *The Inquiry* (2006).

Television has offered Andre Morell in *The Caesars*, George Baker in *I Claudius* and James Mason in *Anno Domini*.

Caligula (AD 37–AD 41)

Caligula, a nickname meaning 'little boot', was named Gaius and managed to rule for only four years. He seems to have been a pretty unspeakable fellow: for a really juicy account read I, Claudius by Robert Graves. He received his just deserts by being murdered by the Praetorian Guard, theoretically the emperor's personal bodyguard, who then proclaimed Caligula's uncle Claudius emperor.

Caligula was played by Emlyn Williams in I Claudius (1937), Jay Robinson in The Robe (1953) and again in its sequel Demetrius and the Gladiators (1954), and Malcolm McDowell in Caligula (1979), which spawned plenty of even more inferior imitations.

For television see Ralph Bates in The Caesars, John Hurt in I Claudius and John McEnery in Anno Domini.

Claudius (AD 41–AD 54)

Claudius engineered the invasion of Britain to exploit its gold, tin and iron reserves in AD 43. He brought rebellious King Caratacus to live as an exile in Rome in AD 51. Eventually he married once too often and was poisoned by his fourth wife, Agrippina II, to secure the empire for her son from a previous marriage, Nero.

On screen Claudius has been portrayed by Charles Laughton in I Claudius (1937), Barry Jones in Demetrius and the Gladiators (1954), Peter Damon in The Fall of the Roman Empire (1964), Giancarlo Badessi in Caligula (1979) and Jack Shepherd in Boudica (2003).

On television he has been played by Freddie Jones in The Caesars and stammering Derek Jacobi in I, Claudius.

Nero (AD 54–AD 68)

Nero succeeded Claudius thanks to his mother Agrippina's efforts. Rivals were quickly dispatched and calm rule was established under Seneca while Nero was young. Soon, however, Nero pursued the arts of singing and dancing, much to the distaste of many. Boudica upset the peace in Britain in AD 61 and there were several plots against the emperor at Rome. In AD 64 a fire destroyed much of Rome; the Christians were blamed, though some thought Nero had started the fire so he could take the opportunity to build his dream golden palace, the *domus aurea* – remains of which can be seen today near the Colosseum in Rome. Nero killed his mother and two of his wives and suffered further revolts against him before committing suicide with the immortal last words '*qualis artifex pereo*' (what an artist the world is losing).

On screen: Charles Laughton in *The Sign of the Cross* (1932), twice by Gino Cervi in *Nerone e Messalina* (1949) and *OK Nerone* (1951), Peter Ustinov in *Quo Vadis* (1951), for which he won an Oscar, Peter Lorre in *The Story of Mankind* (1957), Patrick Cargill in *Up Pompeii* (1971), Dom DeLuise in *History of the World Part I* (1981) and Andrew Lee Potts in *Boudica* (2003).

Television: Martin Potter in *The Caesars*, Christopher Biggins in *I Claudius*, Anthony Andrews in *Anno Domini* and Klaus Maria Brandauer in the mini-series *Quo Vadis*.

The Year of the Four Emperors (AD 68–AD 69)

This year was marked by civil war. Galba didn't last long, being dispatched by the Praetorian Guard. Successor Otho honourably committed suicide and Vitellius fell at the hands of Vespasian.

John Woodvine in *The Caesars* and Roy Purcell in *I, Claudius* have played Vitellius on television.

The names of Vitellius and Vespasian will also be familiar to the readers of Simon Scarrrow's *Eagle* novels.

Vespasianus (AD 69–AD 79)

Vespasian was an old soldier who had campaigned in Britain and

Judaea (the latter a war which led to the sieges and falls of Jersualem in AD 70 and of Masada, along with mass suicide, in AD 73). He notably began the Colosseum and actually managed both to die of natural causes – a rare feat – and produce a famous deathbed quotation, '*vae, puto, deus fio*' – 'Woe (or should that be whoa?), I think I'm turning into a god'. Vespasian also famously uttered, '*necesse est imperatori stanti mori*' – 'It's necessary for an emperor to die standing'.

Lindsey Davis set her Marcus Didius Falco novels during his reign.

Titus (AD 79–AD 81)

The son of Vespasian, Titus had to cope with the eruption of Vesuvius in AD 79, a fire in Rome and the completion of the Colosseum. He most probably died of malaria, and intriguingly observed, 'I have made but one mistake'.

Caroline Lawrence set her series of *The Roman Mysteries* during his reign.

Domitianus (AD 81–AD 96)

Domitian, the younger brother of Titus, was given rather a bad press by contemporary writers. He was assassinated by the Praetorian Guard.

Nerva (AD 96–AD 98)

Nerva managed to live through the reigns of Nero and his successors. By the time he became emperor he was old and childless, so not considered too much of a liability. Nerva died of natural causes two years later.

Norman Wooland remains the only screen Nerva in *Quo Vadis* (1951) though his predecessors are portrayed alongside earlier emperors, for example John Gielgud in *Caligula* (1979).

Traianus (AD 98–AD 117)

The adopted son of Nerva, Trajan celebrated his victory over the Dacians with his famous column. Amedeo Nazarri is the sole Trajan on screen in *Columna* (1968).

Hadrianus (AD 117–AD 138)

Hadrian was widely considered a good egg, the third of the five so-called decent emperors, and he died of natural causes. Parts of his Wall still stand in northern England.

Antoninus Pius (AD 138–AD 161)

He was only pious in the sense that he encouraged Hadrian's deification, but he did manage an impressively long reign. Antoninus Pius also tried to build the Antonine Wall in Britain, to the north of Hadrian's, but it failed to have the longevity of its predecessor. His last word was the password, issued to the inquiring head of the night-watch, deciding upon '*aequanimitas*' – equanimity.

Marcus Aurelius (AD 161–AD 180)

Things now start to get complicated. Aurelius was co-emperor with Lucius Verus for a while, and then again with his son Commodus, possibly leading to the collapse of the *pax Romana*. He was the author of *Meditations* and died of chickenpox.

Alec Guinness played Marcus Aurelius in *The Fall of the Roman Empire* (1964). Richard Harris portrayed him in *Gladiator* (2000).

Commodus (AD 177–AD 192)

Commodus' reign is considered the beginning of the end. He was particularly fond of naked personal gladiatorial combat, and so revolted many of his fellow Romans. He was strangled by a wrestler called Narcissus.

Both Christopher Plummer in *The Fall of the Roman Empire* (1964) and Joaquin Phoenix in *Gladiator* (2000) play Commodus as wonderfully deranged, and they both suffer deaths in hand-to-hand combat. From this age onwards the Roman Empire slowly decayed. Many of the emperors were not particularly well-known to history (certainly Hollywood lost interest); they had easily muddled names such as Constans, Constantius and Constantinus, and met violent deaths, either murdered or killed in battle. The decline was not helped by Diocletian's division of the Empire between East and West in AD 284.

Constantine (AD 306–AD 337)

Constantine stands apart from the later emperors. He was instrumental in ending the persecution of Christians in the empire after defeating Maxentius at the battle of Milvian Bridge in AD 312. Here he is said to have received the divine *'in hoc signo, vinces'* – under the sign (of the cross), you will win. It didn't all go swimmingly for the Christians, however, though Emperor Julian II later admitted (as he died in AD 363), *'vicisti, Galilaee'* – you've won, man of Galilee – after failing to seize back the religious initiative.

Constantine held control of the Eastern Empire and established a new capital at Byzantium, renaming it Constantinople in AD 330. He was portayed by Cornel Wilde in *Constantino il Grande* (1962) and by Robert Vincent Jones in *Nicholas of Myra* (2008).

Rome, capital of the Western Empire, suffered plundering by the Visigoths in 410 and was sacked by the Vandals in 455. The city and its empire effectively ended after Romulus Augustus was forced to resign in 476. However, the Eastern Empire survived for another millennium until the fall of Constantinople in 1453.

A LITTLE BIT OF LATIN
What Have the Romans Ever Done for Us?

One may remember the famous scene in *Monty Python's Life of Brian* in which Reg, leader of the People's Front of Judaea (aka John Cleese), tried to inspire his fellow revolutionaries with an attack on the occupying Romans.

Cleese All right, but apart from the sanitation, medicine, education, wine, public order, irrigation, roads, the fresh water system and public health, what have the Romans ever done for us?
Attendee Brought peace?

Scholars may debate how much of the above is true, but the Romans may certainly be said to have played their part – even if some of these innovations were borrowed from other civilizations. The BBC also borrowed from Monty Python with *What the Romans Did For Us*, a series introduced by Adam Hart-Davis and first aired in 2000. Adding to the list covering aqueducts, baths, pavements, sanitation, firemen, police, street cleaners and laws, they have also been credited with bringing to Britain the Latin language, of course, plus literature, art, architecture, benefits for the poor, street cleaners, parks, public libraries, blocks of flats, public advertisements, the census, glass, coins, cement, bricks, shops, turnips, carrots, cabbage, peas, apples, pears, grapes, cats and, er, stinging nettles. So thanks very much for those.

ROMAN BATHS OR *THERMAE*

The earliest examples of baths were found in Crete and Santorini. Copying the Greeks once again, the Romans expanded their size and spread the culture of baths across the empire. They were known as *balneae* or *thermae*, although *thermae* tended to be used for those connected to warm springs such as those at *Aquae Sulis* (Bath), which remained popular long after the Romans had left Britain. These noisy, cavernous 'leisure centres' were visited daily by the majority of Romans who could not afford costly heating and plumbing systems, while the wealthy minority had their private facilities. Entry was cheap, costing a *quadrans* (smallest coin) in Empire times, when baths were all the rage. The hypocaust system of heating regulated the temperatures of the various rooms.

The *frigidarium* was a room with a cool, at times even frigid swimming pool. The *tepidarium* was a warmish room containing a tepid pool, while the *caldarium* was a sweaty room with a hot pool. Even hotter was the *laconicum*, the room named after the laconic Spartans. This, in effect a sauna, was usually a refuge for invalids.

Bathers changed in the *apodyterium*, leaving their clothes to the mercy of thieves – unless they had brought a slave to guard them. They would exercise in the *palaestra*, which might also contain an outdoor pool. Instead of soap Romans used oil, which was scraped off by a *strigil*. They could also hire masseurs and barbers (*tonsores*).

Pompeii had three sets of baths, while in Herculaneum one can visit two separated for male and female use. The most famous baths of Rome are those of Caracalla, built long after the two towns were buried by Vesuvius. Roman military camps also incorporated baths into their building plans.

JULIUS CAESAR
THE NUMBER ONE MOST FAMOUS ROMAN

Born in 100 BC, Gaius Julius Caesar is the most famous of all Romans, thanks to his military achievements including his invasion of Britain or lack of it, his hairstyle swept forward to cover recession, an affair with Queen Cleopatra of Egypt and a particularly dramatic death, made famous by Shakespeare – though instead of saying 'et tu, Brute', it is thought he said 'και συ, τεκνον' ('and you, [my] child'). He combined his expertise with the wealthy Crassus and the popular Pompey, with whom he shared much power.

Caesar conquered Gaul between 58 BC and 51 BC, but aroused the jealousy of many dangerous rivals in the senate at Rome. When Pompey joined forces against him, Caesar crossed the river Rubicon, thereby declaring civil war and burning his bridges with the highly quotable 'alea iacta est'. After defeating Pompey at Pharsalus in 48 BC, he campaigned in Asia (veni, vidi, vici), Africa and Spain. Since Caesar was then holding extensive offices such as pontifex maximus, consulship and, most importantly, the dictatorship, which was only one step away from emperorship, Brutus, Cassius and others feared for the survival of the Republic. They conspired and assassinated him on 15 March (the Ides of March) 44 BC. Caesar's body, covered in stab wounds, fell dramatically (at least according to Shakespeare) at the base of Pompey's statue.

Some of his writings survive, including the ever-popular de bello Gallico (Gallic Wars) and de bello civili (Civil Wars). From 'Caesar' derive words such as caesarean (his alleged method of birth, probably incorrect), Czar/Tsar and Kaiser – and even, through the town of Xerez, also known as Jerez, the name of the drink sherry.

Caesar has been played numerous times on television, often adapted from Shakespeare, and in the cinema – a spate of sword and sandal Italian epics in the early 1960s have been followed most recently by the live action Asterix films. The list below is a cinematic selection:

Fabrice Luchini *Astérix and Obélix: God Save Britannia* (2012)
Christopher Plummer *Caesar and Cleopatra* (2009)
Alain Delon *Astérix aux Jeux Olympiques* (2008)
Alain Chabat *Astérix and Obélix: Mission Cléopâtra* (2002)
Klaus Maria Brandauer *Vercingetorix* (2001)
John Gottfried *Astérix and Obélix contre César* (1999)
John Gielgud *Julius Caesar* (1970)
Kenneth Williams *Carry On Cleo* (1964)
Alessandro Sperli *Giants of Rome* (1964)
Ivo Garrani *Son of Spartacus* (1963)
Rex Harrison *Cleopatra* (1963)
Cameron Mitchell *Caesar the Conqueror* (1962)
Gustavo Rojo *Julius Caesar against the Pirates* (1962)
Gordon Scott *A Queen for Caesar* (1962)
John Gavin *Spartacus* (1960)
Reginald Sheffield *The Story of Mankind* (1957)
Louis Calhern *Julius Caesar* (1953)
Harold Tasker *Julius Caesar* (1950)
Claude Rains *Caesar and Cleopatra* (1945)
Warren William *Cleopatra* (1934)

ROMAN AUTHORS

This is a short history of those authors worth remembering. They have provided many of the quotations in this book and inspired literature over the last two millennia.

Titus Macius Plautus wrote plays based on Greek comedy, including *The Menaechmi* around 200 BC, and provided Shakespeare with inspiration.

Quintus Ennius paved the way for Latin poetry, despite little of his work surviving.

Publius Terentius Afer (Terence) was a former Carthaginian slave who wrote plays in the 160s BC.

Titus Lucretius wrote six books *de rerum naturae* in the first century BC.

Gaius Valerius Catullus was a poet who flourished in the 50s BC. He is famous for loving and losing Lesbia/Clodia.

Gaius Sallustius Crispus (Sallust) wrote the *bellum Catilinae* and *bellum Iugurthae*.

Marcus Terentius Varro was a contemporary of Caesar's, writing *res rustica* and on language.

Publilius Syrus, an actor of the 40s BC, is credited with numerous maxims.

Gaius Julius Caesar is discussed in his own section (p.124).

Marcus Tullius Cicero (106–43 BC), known as Tully, was a politician and supreme orator. He came to prominence in 70 BC by prosecuting Verres, an unscrupulous governor of Sicily. In 63 BC Cicero was elected consul and suppressed the Catiline conspiracy, executing Catiline without a trial. He was exiled for this in 58 BC, only to be recalled by Pompey a year later. As a staunch supporter of the Republic and status quo, he regretted Pompey's defeat in the civil war (49/8 BC), welcomed Caesar's assassination in 44 BC and proceeded to speak against Antony. When Antony allied himself to Octavian, he had Cicero executed. His head and right hand, symbolizing his speeches and written words, were placed on the *rostrum* (speaker's platform built from the prows of ships) as a warning to others.

Cicero wrote both prosecuting speeches (for example in *Verrem*, *in Catilinam*) and defending ones (*pro Marcello*, *pro Milone*), as well as rhetorical works, philosophy and essays such as *de officiis*, *de amicitia* and *de senectute*. Because so many of his more informal and personal letters survive, Cicero remains one of the more accessible Romans, revealing a human condition as recognizably true today as it was in his lifetime.

Publius Vergilius Maro (Virgil) wrote the 10 *Bucolics* (*Eclogues*) — number four generated much excitement for supposedly predicting the birth of either Christ or Augustus. He also wrote the *Georgics* (four books) and, his *pièce de résistance*, the *Aeneid* (12 books).

Quintus Horatius Flaccus (Horace) fought with Brutus at Philippi. A biography by Suetonius documented his life. He wrote the *Epodes*, *Odes*, *Satires*, *Epistles* and *ars poetica*.

Titus Livius (Livy) was a fan of Cicero. He wrote *ab urbe condita*, consisting of 142 books, of which 35 survive today.

Publius Ovidius Naso (Ovid) was famous for *Metamorphoses* and *fasti*. Augustus exiled him to the Black Sea for writing indecent poems.

Phaedrus, author of fables, was a freedman of Augustus.

Lucius Annaeus Seneca (the Younger) left letters, Stoic philosophy and tragedies. He was forced to commit suicide by Nero.

Gaius Plinius Secundus (Pliny the Elder) wrote *naturalis historia*. He died at Stabiae after the eruption of Vesuvius in AD 79 (pp.130-1).

Gaius Plinius Caecilius Secundus (Pliny the Younger), was adopted by his uncle Pliny. He wrote many letters, several of them to the Emperor Trajan.

Marcus Fabius Quintilianus (Quintilian) produced the *institutio oratoria* on rhetoric and was a big fan of Cicero.

Martial wrote epigrams in the reign of Domitian.

Plutarch wrote biographies on famous Greeks and Romans around AD 100.

Publius Cornelius Tacitus was the son-in-law of Agricola, governor of Britain. He wrote the *Annals* and *Histories*.

Decimus Iunius Iuvenalis (Juvenal) wrote 16 *Satires*. He was the source of many quotable phrases, such as the Romans' sole interest of *panem et circenses*.

Suetonius was a biographer of Caesar and the first 11 emperors. He wrote during Hadrian's reign.

Marcus Aurelius wrote the Stoic *meditationes* while campaigning next to the Danube.

Ambrose was a fourth-century bishop of Milan who composed many religious writings.

Jerome translated the Vulgate Bible from Greek into Latin, completing the work in AD 385.

Claudian was a poet of the late fourth century AD.

Aurelius Augustinus (Augustine) wrote prolifically, including the famous *Confessions*.

Horace, *Odes* 1.4, line 15

vitae summa brevis spem nos vetat incohare longam.

They are not long, the weeping and the laughter,
  Love and desire and hate:
I think they have no portion in us after
  We pass the gate.

They are not long, the days of wine and roses:
  Out of a misty dream
Our path emerges for a while, then closes
  Within a dream.

Ernest Dowson (1867–1900)

THE ERUPTION OF VESUVIUS

What a mercy that Tacitus asked Pliny the Younger, aged only 17 in AD 79, to describe the events surrounding the eruption of the volcano Vesuvius, or more accurately Mount Somma. Pliny's two letters are the only surviving eyewitness account. Tacitus' summary would have been included in his *Annales*, which break off in AD 70 and are therefore lost to posterity.

Tacitus had asked Pliny to outline the circumstances of his uncle Pliny the Elder's death during the disaster. As *praefectus classi* Pliny the Elder was in charge of the local navy. He was stationed at Misenum, about 22 miles west of Somma–Vesuvius across the Bay of Naples in south Italy. On the afternoon of 24 August (a recently discovered coin, struck in October, has revised the date to 24 October) Pliny's attention was brought to a strange cloud in the sky. It was shaped like a Mediterranean umbrella pine, which would be similar to a mushroom cloud, and appeared sometimes white, sometimes dark with earth. Being the writer of *naturalis historia* Pliny was naturally curious, and ordered a boat to be prepared for a closer look. Then, upon receiving a message for help, he switched to quadriremes as his adventure turned into a rescue mission.

They headed straight for the beleaguered shore at the base of the volcano, but the helmsman noted that debris was already blocking the harbour entrance. The party therefore diverted further south to *Stabiae*, now know as Castellammare di Stabia, where Pliny met his friend Pomponianus, who had already loaded ships for escape despite unfavourable winds. Calmly Pliny bathed, dined and stayed the night at Pomponianus' villa, while flames leapt from the volcano some 10 miles to the north-east. By the morning, although still pitch black, ash and pumice stones had fallen all around. The decision was taken to make a run for it and the party made their way to the shore, only to find the waves too wild for safe navigation. As the smell of sulphur increased, Pliny suddenly collapsed. When daylight finally returned on 26 October his body was found, still intact, as if asleep rather than dead.

Catullus, Poem 5, lines 4–6

soles occidere et redire possunt:
nobis, cum semel occidit brevis lux,
nox est perpetua una dormienda.

The sun may set and rise:
But we contrariwise
Sleep after our short light
One everlasting night.

Walter Raleigh (1554–1618)

GODS OF GREECE AND ROME

The Olympians are the gods and goddesses who inhabited Mount Olympus and whom the Romans assimilated into their own organization. The first name is the Greek, the second its Roman equivalent, with their sphere of influence shown in brackets. Note the relationship of the planets in our solar system to several of the Roman names.

Jupiter's father was Saturn/Cronos, his grandfather Uranus and his grandmother Earth/Gaia.

In addition there was Hades (the Roman god Pluto/Dis/Orcus), who governed the underworld of the dead. He did not live on Olympus, and his wife Persephone (Proserpina) spent half the year with him and half with her mother Demeter.

There were several other minor deities. In fact the Romans were keen on having a deity for everything, for example Aeolus (winds), Aura (breeze), Eos (dawn), Eris (discord) and Iris (rainbow). They borrowed the Etruscan idea of worshipping the Lares at *lararia* (household shrines) in their houses, and would certainly have valued Janus (god of the main door) from whom the name January is derived. The Romans continued to import gods as their empire expanded; Pan/Faunus (from Greece), Mithras (Persia) and Isis (Egypt) all fall into this category. They even built the Pantheon in Rome to house all the gods, the meaning of the word in Greek.

Zeus
Jupiter
(sky)

Hera
Juno
(marriage)

Poseidon
Neptune
(sea)

Ares
Mars
(war)

Aphrodite
Venus
(love)

Apollo
Apollo
(sun, music,
prophecy)

Demeter
Ceres
(agriculture)

Hephaestus
Vulcan
(forges)

Hermes
Mercury
(messages)

Athena
Minerva
(wisdom,
war)

Artemis
Diana
(moon,
hunting)

Dionysus
Bacchus
(wine)

who is often
replaced, to give
a 6:6 gender
balance, by

Hestia
Vesta
(hearth, home,
domestic life)

Quiz V
A LITERARY CHALLENGE

Identify these genuine book titles. They have all been freshly translated into Latin, and are surely available from all good bookshops.

vestes novae imperatoris (Hans Christian Andersen)

magus mirabilis in Oz (Frank L. Baum)

nuticulus satyricon (Enid Blyton)

ursus nomine Paddington (Michael Bond)

Alicia in terra mirabili (Lewis Carroll)

Pinoculus liber qui iscribitur (Carlo Collodi)

Rebilius Cruso (Daniel Defoe)

regulus vel pueri soli sapiunt (Antoine de Saint Exupéry)

quomodo invidiosulus nomine Grinchus Christi natalem abrogaverit (Dr Seuss)

aurae inter salices (Kenneth Grahame)

Rumpelstultulus fabula (Brothers Grimm)

Ferdinandus Taurus (Munro Leaf)

Hiawatha (Henry Longfellow)

Winnie ille Pu semper ludet (A. A. Milne)

fundus animalium (George Orwell)

fabula de Petro Cuniculo (Beatrix Potter)

Harrius Potter et philosophi lapis (J. K. Rowling)

arbor alma (Shel Silverstein)

insula thesauraria (R. L. Stevenson)

hobbitus ille (J. R. R. Tolkien)

tela Charlottae (E. B. White)

Answers on page 160

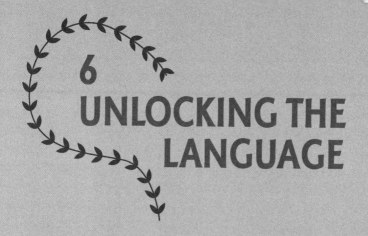

6
UNLOCKING THE LANGUAGE

PARTS OF SPEECH

Latin isn't all fun and games and egomaniacal emperors. When it comes to learning the language, one must understand the complexities that make it so compelling – and sometimes so frustrating. There will be a lot of talk about parts of speech, so here they are.

Parts of Speech	English examples	Latin examples
1. Verb	is, loves	*est, amat*
2. Noun	girl, boy	*puella, puer*
3. Pronoun	she, him	*illa, illum*
4. Adjective	beautiful, my	*pulcher, meus*
5. Adverb	immediately, now	*statim, nunc*
6. Preposition	towards, near	*ad, prope*
7. Conjunction	and, but	*et, sed*
8. Interjection	gosh!	*ecce*
9. Article	a, the	

All words have to be at least one of the above. Some particularly clever ones can be more than one, depending on context.

English grammar is a minefield, so to prevent your brains exploding here's a breakdown of those parts of speech, arguably simplified by a Latin perspective.

I. A VERB describes an action or state

Some are transitive, requiring an object. Others are intransitive, requiring only a subject. The verb is so important it has been given its own section in this book (p.143), but these are the categories one will meet in Latin grammar.

a. **Conjugation** 1st, 2nd, 3rd, 4th, Mixed, Irregular
b. **Person** 1st, 2nd, 3rd
c. **Number** Singular, Plural
d. **Tense** Present, Future Simple, Imperfect, Perfect, Future Perfect, Pluperfect
e. **Mood** Indicative, Subjunctive, Infinitive (Gerund), Imperative, Participle (Gerundive)
f. **Voice** Active, Passive (Deponent)

English has retained most of the above, but uses auxiliary words to come to the rescue.

II. A NOUN names a person or thing

See the separate section on cases below.
a. **Declension** 1st, 2nd, 3rd, 4th, 5th
b. **Case** Nominative, Vocative, Accusative, Genitive, Dative, Ablative, Locative
c. **Number** Singular, Plural
d. **Gender** Masculine, Feminine, Neuter

A noun formed from a verb is either a gerund or an infinitive.

English has done away with these categories apart from singular and plurals, which maintain some formidable exceptions (men cf. talismans, geese cf. mongooses, mice, oxen, stories), and imported many from other languages (for example criteria, seraphim, phenomena, fungi, oases).

III. A PRONOUN replaces a noun
a. **Declension** very individual/unique
b. **Case** same as nouns but no vocative
c. **Number** same as nouns
d. **Gender** same as nouns
e. **Type** Personal, Reflexive, Relative, Demonstrative, Intensive
English has retained all the above to differing extents.

IV. An ADJECTIVE describes a noun
a. **Declension** 1st along with 2nd, 3rd
b. **Case** same as nouns
c. **Number** same as nouns
d. **Gender** same as nouns
e. **Degree** Positive, Comparative, Superlative

An adjective formed from a verb is either a participle or a gerundive.
English adjectives are much simpler though there is still the odd trap (blond, blonde) and they do enjoy degrees.

V. An ADVERB describes a verb
It enjoys the same degrees as an adjective, otherwise it is unchangeable.

VI. A PREPOSITION states the relationship between a noun or a pronoun to something else in the sentence.
It does not alter form. In Latin it governs either the accusative or the ablative. English prepositions change pronouns into the accusative.

VII. A CONJUNCTION joins together two nouns, phrase or sentences.
It does not alter form.

VIII. An INTERJECTION is usually a single word used as an exclamation.
It does not alter form.

IX. An ARTICLE introduces a noun, rather like an adjective, hence the preference of many grammars to number eight parts of speech.

In Latin there is no definite or indefinite article, but there is always the numeral adjective *unus* (one) if necessary. For all the various forms of verbs, nouns, pronouns and adjectives, too numerous to list in one sitting, consult the enduring (and not always beloved) bible of Latin grammar, *Kennedy's Latin Primer*.

EXPLORING CASES

All Latin nouns are in one of seven cases. Adjectives have to follow suit with the nouns with which they agree, and pronouns use up to six cases.

In Latin there is no indefinite or definite article to indicate case (and number and gender) – for example *der, die, das* in German – which can make life very difficult. Latin's several declensions make it worse. However, there is little point in reciting noun declensions until the cases are understood.

English used to have cases, but they have now been largely dropped and survive only in pronouns (e.g. he, him, his; who, whom, whose; they, them, theirs). Here they are called nominative / subjective, accusative/objective and genitive/possessive respectively. Yet this is good news.

We know that 'him was shot' sounds wrong, whereas 'he was shot' is much better – so we have a nominative.

'Me love she' is clearly rubbish, but 'I love her' does the trick. So 'I' is nominative and 'her' is accusative.

Case	Use	Example
Nominative	The Subject of a sentence	Augustus was succeeded by Tiberius.
Vocative	An Addressee	'Do your homework, boy!'
Accusative	Direct Object	I love cats.
	After certain prepositions e.g. *ad, in, prope*	The worm burrowed into the hapless fellow's brain
	Time 'how long' phrase	He rested three days, i.e. for three days.

Genitive	Possession 'of'	Caesar's legions, i.e. the legions of Caesar
Dative	Indirect Object 'to'	I gave to him a tip, i.e. I gave him a tip.
Ablative	After certain prepositions e.g. *a/ab, e/ex, in*	The alien burst out of the tummy. There was a mess in the body.
	Time 'when' phrase	by first light, i.e. at dawn
Locative	locates time, place, state	at/in Rome, at home, in the country, in the evening, at war

Mercifully the ablative subsumed the sociative, also known as the instrumental case.

There are many other cases in other languages. Finnish, for example, enjoys the Partitive, Inessive, Elative, Translative, Instructive, Abessive, Comitative, Illative, Adessive, Allative, Essive and Exessive. Most are achieved by doing away with prepositions and having several variations of the Locative. Hungarian has 35 cases while *The Guinness Book of Records* attributes 48 cases to Tabassaran, a language of Daghestan, found on the west coast of the Caspian Sea.

A LITTLE BIT OF LATIN
A Complex Case

The locative caused some confusion in *Monty Python's Life of Brian* (p.21). The Roman centurion, played by John Cleese, insists that in the phrase 'Romans, go home', the word 'home' is motion towards (correct, as in 'go to home', as we would understand it in English) and locative. Not so – it's not 'at home'. Names of towns, small islands and a few select words just omit the prepositions, but the case is still sustained. So 'to Rome' is *Romam* (accusative) and 'from Rome' is *Roma* (ablative); only 'at Rome' is *Romae* (locative).

THE GRAMMAR OF A VERB

A verb is a pretty essential part of speech as a whole sentence revolves around it. Unfortunately it attracts some of the most complicated grammar.

Here is one of those tables – at the risk of provoking tears of nostalgia from some readers.

amo	I love / am loving
amas	you love / are loving, thou lovest
amat	he / she / it loves / is loving / loveth
amamus	we love / are loving
amatis	you love / are loving, ye love
amant	they love / are loving

Yes, I have been slightly mischievous and put in a few archaic English forms, but it does go to show that verb endings are a necessary evil – as well as useful for appreciating Shakespeare. And really the most important verb, as in all languages, is *esse* (to be).

sum	I am
es	you are, thou art
est	he is, she is, it is, there is
sumus	we are
estis	you are
sunt	they are, there are

amo is...
1st Person (hence the 'I' rather than 'you' or 'he')
Singular ('I' rather than 'we')
Present (happening now)
Indicative (fact)

A *VADE MECUM* OF VERB PARTS

Mood	Person	Number	Tense
Indicative	1,2,3	both	all 6
Subjunctive	1,2,3	both	all except Future
Infinitive			Pres, Fut, Perf
Gerund			
Imperative	2,3	both	Pres, Fut
Participle		both	Pres, Fut, Perf
Gerundive			

Voice	Case	Gender
both	(Nom)	only if using 4th principal part
both	(Nom)	
both	Nom, Acc	neuter
Act	all 6	mostly neuter
both		
both	all 6	all 3
Pass	all 6	all 3

Active (the subject is instigating the action of the verb)
1st Conjugation (it has a lot of 'a's)

And sum is the same, except that its conjugation is irregular.

So a verb has a choice of:

Person	1st, 2nd, 3rd
Number	Singular, Plural
Tense	Present, Future Simple, Imperfect, Perfect, Future Perfect, Pluperfect
Mood	Indicative, Subjunctive, Infinitive (Gerund), Imperative, Participle (Gerundive)
Voice	Active, Passive (Deponent)
Conjugation	1st, 2nd, 3rd, 4th, Mixed, Irregular

'Person' and 'Number' are just like English.

Tensed for Action

Tense is like English, too, but English has about 12 of these. So Latin is simpler in that respect – though it can be argued this can mean loss of a certain precision. Here are the English tenses, illustrated by the verb 'to send', but arranged as Latin would with adverbs to find the correct time scale, and only in the indicative (most common) mood.

Present now I send / am sending / am sent / am being sent
Future Simple soon I shall send / shall be sending / shall be sent
Imperfect often in the past I was sending / used to send / was being sent
Perfect once or twice in the past I sent / have sent / did send / was sent / have been sent
Future Perfect by tomorrow I shall have sent / shall have been sent
Pluperfect a long time ago I had sent / had been sent

Understanding Mood

The term is used loosely to simplify things here, as mood can cause the most upsets.

Indicative is fact I send / I send a letter
Subjunctive is conjecture I may send / I may send a letter
Infinitive is a verbal noun to send / I want to send a letter
Gerund is a verbal noun the sending / the sending of a letter is very important
Imperative is used to give an order send! send a letter!
Participle is an adjectival noun sending / I saw her sending a letter
Gerundive is an adjectival noun must be sent / The letter must be sent

What makes moods complicated is that they come in various persons, numbers, tenses *et cetera*. The table on pages 144-5 above features a checklist of what is available for each mood. It may prove a useful *vade mecum*.

The Voice

Active is when the subject instigates the verb's action   I love

Passive is when the subject suffers the verb's action   I am loved

Deponent is a Latin-only voice, used where the verb has Passive forms but translates as Active.

Creative Conjugation

Latin has four conjugations (i.e. the various forms in order), traditionally represented by *amo, moneo, rego* and *audio*, a mixed one and a few irregulars. A regular verb has about 140 endings.

All verbs are supplied with its own principal parts, e.g. *amo, amare, amavi, amatum* or more spectacularly *tollo, tollere, sustuli, sublatum*: I raise.

Conjugation matters for the first three tenses only. The first two principal parts provide the stem, so for the above example, they'll all start *toll–*.

For the last three tenses, the third principal part provides the stem in the active, so *sustul–*, and the fourth principal part provides the stem in the Passive, so *sublat–*.

Now it is just a question of mastering the endings. Back to *Kennedy's Latin Primer*.

English has one conjugation, a few endings and its own set of principal parts. Its most irregular verb is 'to be'. This verb is irregular in all languages – even Turkish, where it is the only one.

On the other side of the coin a Minnesotan Native American language has up to 6000 verb forms. Various Inuit-Aleutian languages blur the difference between nouns and verbs with hundreds of inflexions.

SELECTED FURTHER READING

S. R. H. James, *Latin I, Latin II, Latin III*, Able Publishing 1998–2016

Simon R. H. James, *London Movie Location Guide*, Batsford 2010

F. M. Wheelock, *Wheelock's Latin*, HarperCollins 1994

R. Colebourn, *Latin Sentence and Idiom*, Bristol Classical Press 1987

B. H. Kennedy and J. Mountford, *Kennedy's Revised Latin Primer*, Longman 1994

S. A. Handford and M. Herberg, *Langenscheidt's Shorter Latin Dictionary*, Hodder and Stoughton 1966

British Hit Singles and Albums, Guinness 2006

Winston S. Churchill, *My Early Life: A Roving Commission*, Mandarin 1991

Nicholas Ostler, AD Infinitum *A Biography of Latin*, HarperPress 2007

Harry Mount, *Amo, Amas, Amat… And All That*, Short Books 2007

Caroline Lawrence, *The Roman Mysteries* series, Orion 2001–2009

Conn Iggulden, *The Emperor* series, HarperCollins 2003–2009

Robert Graves, *I Claudius* and *Claudius The God*, Penguin Classics 2006

Goscinny & Uderzo, *The Adventures of Asterix* series, Orion

Peter Kessler, *Complete Guide to Asterix*, Distribooks, 1997

J. K. Rowling, *The Harry Potter* series, Bloomsbury 1997–2007

John Gray, *Lawyer's Latin*, Robert Hale 2002

John Gray, *Long Live Latin*, Canis Press 2004

Russell Ash, *The Top Ten of Everything 2007*, Hamlyn 2007

Lindsey Davis, *The Falco* series, Random House 1989–2007

Richard Fortey, *Dry Store Room No 1*, Harper Press 2008

Paul Sterry, *Complete British Wildlife*, HarperCollins 1997

Philip Matyszak, *Ancient Rome on Five Denarii on a Day*, Thames and Hudson 2007

James Renshaw, *In Search of the Romans*, Bristol Classical Press 2012

Mary Beard, SPQR, Profile 2015

Websites

There are thousands of internet sites, begging for a Googling.
You could start with, for example;

roman-emperors.org
museumoflondon.org.uk
onlineuniversities.com
wheelockslatin.com
latinlanguage.org
areena.yle.fi1-1931339 for the Nuntii Latini
vatican.va/latin/latin_index.html
asterix.openscroll.org/books
inrebus.com
YouTube tutorials

QUIZ ANSWERS

Quiz I The Best of 00VII (pp.36-37)

medicus minime: doctor at the very least, i.e. Dr No

a sinistra civitate (cum) amore: from the left state with love, i.e. From Russia With Love

digitus auri: finger of gold, i.e. Goldfinger

globus tonitrus: ball of thunder, i.e. Thunderball

bis solum vivis: You Only Live Twice

regius locus in quo ludi pecuniae tenentur: royal place in which games of money are being held, i.e. Casino Royale

in servitudine secreto pro regina (I.S.S.P.R.): in secret service on behalf of the queen, i.e. On Her Majesty's Secret Service

pretiosae lapides sunt aeternae: precious stones are eternal, i.e. Diamonds Are Forever

vivet et moriatur: let him live and die, i.e. Live And Let Die

vir aureo telo: The Man With The Golden Gun

explorator qui me amabat: The Spy Who Loved Me

vir qui lunae imaginem removere conatur, i.e. is qui impossibile somnium petit: the man who tries to remove the image of the moon, i.e. he who seeks an impossible dream, i.e. Moonraker

tuis oculis solum: For Your Eyes Only

animal cui sunt octo membra: animal to which there are eight limbs, i.e. Octopussy

numquam dic numquam iterum: Never Say Never Again

consilium AD necandum/interficiendum: A View To A Kill

vivae luces diei: The Living Daylights

ei licet ut necet/occidat/interficiat: Licence To Kill

oculus aureus: GoldenEye

cras numquam morietur: Tomorrow Never Dies

orbis terrarum haud satis est: The World Is Not Enough

morere alio die: Die Another Day

regius locus in quo ludi pecuniae tenentur: Casino Royale (again)

minima quantitas solacii: a very small quantity of solace, i.e. Quantum Of Solace

e caelo casus: fall from sky, i.e. Skyfall

larva/idolon/umbra: ghost/image, i.e. Spectre

Quiz II Number One Hits (pp.64–67)

1953 *credo*: I Believe

1954 *tres denarii in fonte*: Three Coins In the Fountain

1955 *'liberatum e vinculis' carmen*: 'freed from chains' song, Unchained Melody

1956 *est paene cras*: It's Almost Tomorrow

1957 *erit ille dies [in quo moriar]*: That'll Be The Day [That I Die]

1958 *magni globi ignis*: Great Balls Of Fire

1959 *quid vis?*: What Do You Want?

1960 *solum soli*: Only The Lonely

1961 *ad me recta redi*: return to me directly, Walk Right Back

1962 *terra mira*: Wonderful Land

1963 *quomodo id efficis?*: How Do You Do It?

1964 *domus solis orientis*: House Of The Rising Sun; *magnopere cepisti*: you've captured me greatly, i.e. You Really Got Me

1965 *i nunc*: Go Now; *mihi non satis est*: it's not enough for me, i.e. (I Can't Get No) Satisfaction

1966 *hae caligae factae sunt AD ambulandum*: These Boots Are Made For Walking; *viridianae herbae domi*: Green Green Grass Of Home

1967 *hoc est meum carmen*: This Is My Song; *libera me*: Release Me; *silentium est aureum*: Silence Is Golden

1968 *quam orbem mirabilem* (2007): What A Wonderful World; *mihi tibi nuntiandum est*: I've Gotta Get A Message To You; *parvo auxilio ab meis amicis* (1988; 2004): With A Little Help From My Friends

1969 *quo vadis, mea pulchra?*: Where Do You Go To My Lovely?

1970 *omnia genera omnium*: All Kinds Of Everything; *anulus auri*: Band Of Gold

1971 *calidus amor*: Hot Love

1972 *sine te* (1994): Without You; *quomodo confirmari possum?*: How Can I Be Sure?

1973 *flava vitta antiquam quercum circumligate*: Tie A Yellow Ribbon Round The Old Oak Tree

1974 *illa*: She; *quando iterum te videbis?*: When Will I See You Again?

1975 *si*: If; *navigo*: Sailing

1976 *retine mihi omnia basia*: Save All Your Kisses For Me

1977 *itaque iterum vincis*: So You Win Again

1978 *ter femina*: Three Times A Lady; *aetatis noctes*: Summer Nights

1979 *clari oculi*: Bright Eyes; *nuntius in amphora*: Message In A Bottle

1980 *victor omnia vincit*: The Winner Takes It All

1981 *mulier*: Woman; *nonne me cupis?*: Don't You Want Me?

1983 *verus*: True

1984 *sciuntne diem natalem esse?* (1989, 2004): Do They Know It's Christmas?

1985 *volo scire quid sit amor*: I Want To Know What Love Is; *move propius*: Move Closer

1986 *noli relinquere me hoc modo*: Don't Leave Me This Way

1987 *iterum vincis*: You Win Again; *quis est illa puella?*: Who's That Girl?

1988 *is non gravis est, ille est meus frater*: He Ain't Heavy He's My Brother; *tibi nihil debeo*: I Owe You Nothing; *perfectus*: Perfect; *Olympus est locus, qui est in terra*: Heaven Is A Place On Earth

1989 *aeterna flamma* (2001): Eternal Flame

1990 *nihil te assimulat*: Nothing Compares 2 U

1991 *omnia quae facio, pro te ago*: (Everything I Do) I Do It For You

1992 *finis viae*: End Of The Road; *te semper amabo*: I Will Always Love You

1994 *ubique est amor*: Love Is All Around; *mane alium diem*: Stay Another Day

1995 *villa*: Country House

1996 *noli respectare, irate*: Don't Look Back In Anger; *tres leones* (1998): Three Lions; *vis esse*: you want to be, i.e. Wannabe; *verba*: Words

1997 *noli loqui*: Don't Speak; *candela in vento*: Candle In The Wind; *numquam umquam*: Never Ever

1998 *cor meum supererit*: My Heart Will Go On

1999 *volans sine alis*: Flying Without Wings

2000 *eheu ... iterum egi*: Oops... I Did It Again

2002 *si cras numquam adveniat*: If Tomorrow Never Comes

2003 *pulchra*: Beautiful

2004 *tibi faveo*: I give favour to you, i.e. I'll Stand By You

2005 *adeone Amarillo?*: am I going to Amarillo, i.e. Is This The Way To Amarillo; *es bella*: You're Beautiful; *me tollis*: You Raise Me Up

2006 *mihi ridendum est*: I have to smile, Smile; *mihi saltare non placet*: it's not pleasing for me to dance, i.e. I Don't Feel Like Dancing

2007 *quingenta milia passuum*: five hundred thousands of paces, i.e. 500 Miles; *fortior*: Stronger

2008 *clementia*: Mercy; *illud non est mihi nomen*: That's Not My Name; *curre*: Run

2009 *pueri puellaeque*: Boys And Girls; *os sine expressione*: face without expression, i.e. Poker Face

2010 *scripta in stellis*: Written In The Stars

2011 *aliquis similis tibi*: Someone Like You

2012 *aliquis quem sciebam*: Someone That I Used To Know

2013 *suffusae ligneae*: Blurred Lines; *incende*: Burn; *clama ut leo fremit*: shout as a lion growls, i.e. Roar; *altissima aedes*: very high building, i.e. Skyscraper

2014 *laetus*: Happy; *canta*: Sing

2015 *detrahe me*: Drag Me Down; *quid dicere vis?*: what do you wish to say, i.e. What Do You Mean?

Quiz III Famous Films in Latin (pp.86-87)

Albus Niveus cum septem pumilionibus: Snow White And The Seven Dwarfs

egressus vento: Gone With The Wind

casa alba: white house, Casablanca

femina scelesta: The Wicked Lady

tertius vir: The Third Man

caerulea lucerna: The Blue Lamp

bellum mundorum: War Of The Worlds

medicus adest: a doctor is present, Doctor In The House

et ego et rex: The King and I

decem imperia: The Ten Commandments

circum orbem terrarum octoginta diebus: Around The World In Eighty Days

dormiens pulchra puella: The Sleeping Beauty

Maris undecim: eleven of Sea, Ocean's Eleven

superbi septem: proud seven, The Magnificent Seven

centum et uni canes: 101 Dalmatians

iuvenes: The Young Ones

trecenti [Lacedaemonii]: The 300 Spartans/ just called 300 in 2006

longissima dies: The Longest Day

mea pulchra femina: My Fair Lady

iuva!: Help!

sonitus carminum: The Sound Of Music

ubi aquilae audent: Where Eagles Dare

o, iecur! (!): o liver, Oliver!

fabula amoris: Love Story

vir qui obtulit aliquid quod non recusandum erat: the man who offered something which was not to be refused, i.e. The Godfather

sellae equitationis incandescentes: incandescent seats of equitation, i.e. Blazing Saddles

turris ignis: tower of fire, i.e. The Towering Inferno

dentes maris: teeth of the sea, i.e. Jaws

bella stellarum : spes nova: Star Wars: A New Hope

pons plus: A Bridge Too Far

ea quae non nata est in terra: she which has not been born on earth, i.e. Alien

imperium repugnat: The Empire Strikes Back

currus ignis: Chariots Of Fire

id quod non natum est in terra: it which has not been born on earth, i.e. ET
    (whose gender is never specified)

redite AD futurum: Back To The Future

optima hasta (!): excellent spear, i.e. Top Gun

improba saltatio: wicked dance, i.e. Dirty Dancing

ultimum iter pro bono: ultimate journey on behalf of good, i.e. (Indiana Jones
    and The) Last Crusade

vir qui est similis mammali noctis: man who is similar to a mammal of the night,
    i.e. Batman

domi solus: Home Alone

femina pulchra: Pretty Woman

silentium agnorum: Silence Of The Lambs

hortus antiquorum animalium: garden of ancient animals, i.e. Jurassic Park

quattuor nuptiae funusque unum: Four Weddings and a Funeral

leo regius: royal lion, i.e. The Lion King

Romanus deus solis, tredecim: Roman god of the sun 13, i.e. Apollo 13

maxima navis quae summersa est: very great ship which sank, i.e. Titanic

viri in vestibus nigris: men in black clothes, i.e. Men in Black

scriptor notus in amore: famous writer in love, i.e. Shakespeare In Love

mater (!): mother, i.e. The Mummy

non in colle (!): not in the hill, i.e. Notting Hill

sextus sensus: The Sixth Sense

illa quae feminae cupiunt: What Women Want

conveniamus parentes: let's meet the parents, i.e. Meet The Parents

cubiculum celatarum rerum: room of hidden things, i.e. (Harry Potter And The)
    Chamber Of Secrets

de puero: About A Boy

heros araneus: Spider-Man

rex redit: king returns, i.e. The Return of the King (The Lord Of The Rings)

inveniens 'no-one': Finding Nemo

amor re vera: Love Actually

arca mortui: Dead Man's Chest (Pirates Of The Caribbean)

laeti pedes: Happy Feet

ludi senioris carmina: songs of the senior school, i.e. High School Musical

expiatio: Atonement

crepesculum: Twilight

eques obscura: The Dark Knight

mea mater: Mamma Mia!

iter per stellas: journey through stars, i.e. Star Trek

inceptio: Inception

regis oratio: The King's Speech

celer quinque: Fast Five

miseri: Les Misérables

gravitas: Gravity

frigidissimus: very cold, i.e. Frozen

proelium quinque exercituum: Battle Of Five Armies (The Hobbit)

quinquaginta glauci colores: Fifty Shades Of Grey

qui e mortuis rediit: he who returned from the dead, i.e. The Revenant

Quiz IV Number One Pop Artists (pp.110–111)

1954 *porta est dies* (!): door is day, i.e. Doris Day

1956 *textores somniorum*: weavers of dreams, i.e. The Dreamweavers

1957 *cicadae*: The Crickets

1958 *semper pratum fratres*: always lea brothers, i.e. The Everly Brothers

1961 *umbrae*: The Shadows

1963 *exquisitores*: The Searchers

1964 *animalia*: The Animals; *saxa volventia*: The Rolling Stones

1965 *fratres iusti*: The Righteous Brothers; *petitores*: The Seekers; *ilices aquifoliae*: The Hollies; *aves*: The Byrds; *apricus et divide* (!): sunny and share, i.e. Sonny and Cher

1966 *fratres qui ambulant*: brothers who walk, i.e. The Walker Brothers; *vultus parvi*: The Small Faces; *pueri litoris*: boys of the beach, i.e. The Beach Boys

1967 *simii qui litteras ordinare non possunt*: simians who can't spell, i.e. The Monkees

1971 *aurora*: Dawn; *media via*: Middle of the Road; *necatus*: killed/slayed, i.e. Slade

1972 *novi petitores*: The New Seekers

1973 *decem vide vide* (!): ten see see, i.e. 10CC

1974 *limus*: Mud; *tres adiunctivae quantitates*: three adjectival quantities, i.e. The Three Degrees

1975 *regina*: Queen

1976 *hiems, ver, aestas, autumnus*: winter spring summer autumn, i.e. The Four Seasons; *res vera*: The Real Thing

1977 'lion' orator: Leo Sayer; *alae*: Wings

1979 *vicani incolae*: inhabitants of the village, i.e. Village People; *vigiles*: nightwatchmen, i.e. The Police

1981 *primus vir et formicae*: first man and ants, i.e. Adam and the Ants; *hominum foedus*: treaty/league of mankind, i.e. Human League

1983 *currisne? currisne?*(!): do you run? do you run?, i.e. Duran Duran;

tu, *age quadraginta:* You act 40, i.e. UB40

1987　*stellarum navis:* ship of the stars, i.e. Starship

1988　*madidus umidus udus:* Wet Wet Wet; *tu quoque:* you too, i.e. U2

1989　*novi iuvenes in via:* new young men on the street, i.e. New Kids on the
　　　　Block; *animi stulti:* Simple Minds

1990　*australis pulcher:* The Beautiful South

1992　*a pueris* AD *viros:* from boys to men, i.e. Boyz II Men

1993　*tene illud:* Take That

1994　*princeps:* Prince

1995　*arbores circum aquam in deserto:* trees around water in a desert, i.e. Oasis

1996　*puellae cibi acris:* girls of bitter food, i.e. Spice Girls

1998　*totaliter beatae:* totally blessed females, i.e. All Saints

1999　*gradus:* Steps; *Britannum genu, hastae:* British knee spears, i.e. Britney
　　　　Spears

2002　*dulces infantes* or perhaps *mellis bellissimae:* sweet babies or perhaps very
　　　　beautiful females of honey, i.e. The Sugababes

2003　*fractus:* broken, i.e. Busted; *proclivis restire* (!): liable to bounce,
　　　　bouncey, i.e. Beyoncé

2004　*viae:* The Streets

2009　*femina insane* (!): mad woman, i.e. Lady Gaga

2010　*flue, eques:* flow rider, i.e. Flo Rida

2011　*exemplum:* Example; *valles* (!): a valley/dell, i.e. Adele

2012　*florea et machine:* Florence And The Machine

2013　*auferens stultus:* stealing stupid, i.e. Robin Thicke; *voluntas.ego.sum:*
　　　　Will.i.am

2015　*paulum mixtae:* mixed a little, i.e. Little Mix

Quiz V A Literary Challenge (pp.134–135)

vestes novae imperatoris: The Emperor's New Clothes

magus mirabilis in Oz: The Wonderful Wizard of Oz

nuticulus satyricon: Noddy and the Goblins

ursus nomine Paddington: A Bear Called Paddington

Alicia in terra mirabili: Alice in Wonderland

Pinoculus liber qui iscribitur: Pinocchio

Rebilius Cruso: Robinson Crusoe

regulus vel pueri soli sapiunt: The Little Prince

quomodo invidiosulus nomine Grinchus Christi natalem abrogaverit: How the Grinch
    Stole Christmas

aurae inter salices: The Wind in the Willows

Rumpelstultulus fabula: Rumplestiltskin

Ferdinandus Taurus: Ferdinand

Hiawatha: Hiawatha

Winnie ille Pu semper ludet: The House at Pooh Corner

fundus animalium: Animal Farm

fabula de Petro Cuniculo: The Tale of Peter Rabbit

Harrius Potter et philosophi lapis: Harry Potter and the Philosopher's Stone

arbor alma: The Giving Tree

insula thesauraria: Treasure Island

hobbitus ille: The Hobbit

tela Charlottae: Charlotte's Web